BEYOND SOLSTICE GATES

Ahelia Publishing
Helena, Montana

PERFIDY OF LABYRINTH

BY Kimm Reid

BEYOND SOLSTICE GATES

Where the only
way forward is
all the way back

Perfidy of Labyrinth

Second Edition 2018

ISBN- 978-0-9947328-9-7

1. Supernatural 2. Science Fiction 3. Fiction

Published by Ahelia Publishing, LLC.
Printed in the United States of America

www.aheliapublishing.com
kimm.reid@outlook.com

TABLE OF CONTENTS

Gray Eyes Staring

Whatever it was that today might bring, Jennifer expected it would be perfectly marvelous even though it was winter; her least favorite season. It took only minutes outside to remind everyone who may have forgotten that this was a dreadfully cold winter. Nearly everyone, however, was entirely unaware that whatever cold lingered outside had silently crept inside. It was evident to the twins, though, that since they had returned from Trilleah many months before, their little yellow house nestled gently on the corner of Fairview Lane and Mitchell Avenue, felt different. "Chilly," was the only word either of the twins could find to describe the dreadful icy feeling that hung in the air inside their home.

No matter how high they turned the heat or how many logs they threw into the fireplace, the chill hovered in every nook and cranny. It draped itself above their heads; it slithered beneath their feet.

Nevertheless, cold or not-so-cold, winter and all, today would undoubtedly prove to be an unforgettably brilliant sort of day. Jennifer was convinced of this, since today Jennifer and Judah would turn thirteen.

"Finally," Jennifer would say to Judah and he, in his usual fashion, would roll his eyes and respond with a quiet grin and turned up nose. He hated showing emotion of any sort—especially to his sister.

Surprisingly, Bella was throwing them a party. Even better than a party, at least in Jennifer's mind, was that she was *finally* a teenager. Judah didn't seem to care one iota what number of years was attached to him. He couldn't see how thirteen would be any better than twelve. He wasn't too interested in growing up at all, it seemed.

Nevertheless, for Jennifer, the best gift she could receive on this day was the number that would be iced onto the top of her birthday cake. It would say thirteen. And, unlike Judah in all his childish silliness, Jennifer DID want to grow up. After all, teenagers were practically grown-ups and could do almost anything they wanted to, whenever they wanted to do them. Teenagers did not need permission for every little thing. They could stay up late and choose when they went to bed.

In Jennifer's mind, this day would most certainly, without a doubt, absolutely, categorically, entirely, change everything.

As excitement danced through her mind, something else showed up briefly as well. Like the flash from a camera—there one minute and gone the next—a pair of hollow gray eyes appeared from inside of her mind. They appeared and vanished so quickly that it did not even dawn on Jennifer what she had seen. But then, a moment or two later, they appeared again and stayed a bit longer. Like a blink or a light being switched on and off, the eyes were looking at Jennifer, but from the inside, not the outside.

They were hard to focus on since they were nearly fully covered by something—a veil perhaps—and there was no face that she could see; only large, piercing gray eyes.

Jennifer shuddered and closed her own eyes, trying to find them again, and figure out where they'd come from. When she looked for them, they were nowhere to be found. Jennifer shook her head and put the sight out of her mind, convincing herself that she had imagined the outrageously foolish thing.

Probably because I'm so excited about the party, my imagination is going overboard, she thought to herself and chuckled nervously under her breath. She knew it wasn't the truth but sometimes, when things bigger than us are unexplainable, we make up unreasonable explanations; this is precisely what Jennifer did.

"Only 2:00," she mumbled as she glanced at the clock. *Tick, tick, tick,* it cried out loudly. "Only a few more hours until the party." She giggled and did a little spin right there in the kitchen, bumping into a chair and nearly knocking both herself and the chair over. It only made her giggle more.

Nothing would deflate her happiness today ... nothing.

"Enjoy your birthday, sweet Jennifer, because it will surely be the last birthday you ever see!" she heard. A voice, somehow attached to those eyes, was mocking her. The eyes flashed again ... blinked maybe ... and she thought she felt a finger run down her spine, even though she told herself it was just a chill from the icy air. Jennifer debated between running to Bella or believing that what she was seeing and hearing and feeling was only her imagination.

That had to be it. She was so excited that her imagination was going too fast and having outlandish conversations of its own. Again, she decided to pretend that she had not seen, nor heard, anything out of the ordinary. Straightaway she went back to daydreaming on this most wonderful of days, although she was greatly distracted by what she was pretending not to notice.

Yesterday she knew nothing of tonight's party. In fact, she had begun to wonder if Bella had forgotten it even WAS their birthday. But this morning, to Jennifer's surprise, when she woke and found her bedroom door closed, she knew that Bella was up to something. Her door was never closed. Not ever.

After that frightful night with the dark shadows a few months earlier, Jennifer made sure her door stayed open. "If they come back, I do NOT want to be caught behind any closed doors," she reasoned. Bella agreed, and never tried to convince Jennifer otherwise ... until today.

Now that she was a teenager, she may have to rethink the entire door situation because, after all, teenagers are expected to demand their privacy and stay behind closed doors for hours. She wasn't sure what she was supposed to do behind a closed door, but it would come to her, she was sure.

The dark shadows had not returned to her room since before the last Solstice, and by now she was confident that whatever Bella had done to make them leave, had worked well. Any dark shadows that had remained were sure to stay hidden in the privacy of her mind from then until now.

This morning when she opened her eyes to find the door had been closed, however, Jennifer was certain that Bella was up to something. She climbed from her bed, threw on her old, raggedy blue housecoat, and silently popped the door open just a crack. Jennifer closed one eye and peeked through the crack with the other.

"Happy birthday, J," Bella squealed as she padded down the hallway toward her niece. "I thought you'd never get up. But, then again, you ARE a teenager now, so I DO suppose I'll never see you before noon on weekends." Bella smiled and gave Jennifer a tight hug and a warm kiss on the forehead.

"Come with me," Bella said, grabbing Jennifer's hand. She led her to the living room where Judah was already watching television. "Since you're finally awake," Bella said, "I'm excited to tell you both that at precisely 5:00 this afternoon, you will be having twenty guests arriving for a party and pizza and presents."

The twins both gasped, and excitement took over the whole room. Never had the twins been given such extravagance. It was rare that Bella allowed them to have even one friend over. But twenty?! Did they even have twenty friends?

"Go to the kitchen," Bella squealed. "Breakfast is waiting." A mischievous grin peeked from her lips, as she was quite proud of her achievements this morning.

Jennifer was so surprised by all of these happenings that she couldn't think of anything to say. She just looked at Judah, who looked right back, and they all sauntered toward the kitchen quite bewildered at all of these birthday extravagances. Jennifer tried keeping her mind on the things in front of her eyes in an attempt to avoid seeing what was becoming clearer and clearer behind her eyes … those gray staring eyes full of hollow darkness and threats of no more birthdays.

I guess Auntie didn't forget, was all Jennifer could make her mind think. She tried to refuse the eyes a place in her thoughts, but it was getting harder and harder. Those dark eyes that insisted on peering out from somewhere behind her own were throwing her off more than she cared to admit. As hard as Jennifer tried to pretend she didn't see them, it was becoming evident that these intruding eyes were not going to leave her alone anytime soon.

Her thoughts were suddenly interrupted by her brother's booming voice. "What's for breakfast?" he asked. Judah sounded like he was trying to hold in any excitement that may try to seep out and prove that he did, in fact, have emotions. He did like to act as if nothing was ever a big deal to him.

"Well, you'll just have to get yourself into the kitchen and find out," Bella replied.

She was obviously enjoying her little surprises more than either Judah or Jennifer were at this point. However, as they entered the kitchen and their eyes saw what Bella had prepared for breakfast, the twins both became a little less grouchy and a lot more hungry. Smiles stretched across their faces and hung there for quite a few seconds.

"My favorite," Jennifer whispered.

She skipped toward the table and pulled out her chair. Judah did the same ... without the skipping, of course. Spread before them on Mamma's fanciest red cloth-covered table were three large plates of steaming hot French toast with the biggest blobs of butter still in the process of melting. The icing sugar had been sprinkled on perfectly and the syrup was thick, just how syrup was meant to be.

There were many delighted squeals and murmurings of how marvelous thirteen was already turning out to be. Jennifer took a big breath, inhaling the delicious smell of hot butter and melting sugar. Judah did the same. They both closed their eyes and let their nostrils fill up, holding it all inside for a moment.

The twins, exhaling and opening their eyes, took the biggest bites of French toast ever; Judah's much bigger than Jennifer's, of course. Jennifer again closed her eyes as she completely enjoyed every bit of this moment. Judah gobbled down his toast as quickly as he could shove it into his mouth, but Jennifer took a long time to finish hers.

"Thank you, Auntie," she muttered, trying not to let any bits tumble from her mouth. They both laughed and Jennifer brought her hand up just as a few wayward pieces launched out of her mouth and flew across the table. They laughed some more.

"Ya thanks, Auntie," Judah hollered over his shoulder as he sped from the kitchen toward the basement.

"Who's coming to the party?" Jennifer asked. "I don't even know twenty people."

Bella, not wishing to give away any surprises just yet, shrugged the question off. "Well, let me see," she said, tapping her bottom lip with one of her fingers as though she was thinking hard.

"There's James, Ryan, and Luke, of course, from down the street and, hmm, who else is coming," she said, obviously playing some ridiculous sort of game and thinking herself to be quite amusing. "Oh yes! Jayda, Kaitlyn, Kennedy, and Mackenzie from your class will be here as well."

Bella didn't seem to want to give any more information than that, and as much as Jennifer asked about this person or pried about that friend, it was clear that Bella was going to be stubborn and keep some secrets.

"OK," Jennifer answered. "I'll just wait and see." She set her plate carefully into the sink and headed down the hallway, excited to see who would show up later but annoyed that she had to be patient. Patience was not Jennifer's favorite thing.

Tic-Toc Goes the Clock

Now Jennifer, being thirteen and all, was no more patient than when she was six. She looked at the clock for the hundredth time since breakfast and saw only ten minutes had passed since the ninety-ninth time she'd looked at the clock.

"Oh bother," she huffed.

She was able to find the odd thing here and there to keep her busy as she waited for time to pass, but she was becoming much too excited and even a bit nervous ... too nervous to keep her mind on anything for more than just a few minutes. No matter what she did, her mind kept going back to the possibilities of guests whom Bella was keeping secret.

A chill twisted around her skin; she looked to see if the door had been left open. It hadn't, but the noticeable chill left her a bit concerned. Unwelcomed fear snuck in just then.

She tried watching some television, but nothing kept her attention. She shuffled some books around and paged through this one or that one, but none begged to be read.

I'll clean my room, she giggled. *That should take hours.*

Jennifer tidied her desk and folded a few items of clothing from the mound that lay in a heap on the floor but became bored with that too. She looked at her bed, searching for her red blanket, and found it hidden beneath her enormous collection of stuffed bears. She'd had some of those bears since before she could even remember, but since she was thirteen now, decided that maybe she no longer needed them all—at least not all on her bed.

"Well, that won't do," she told the bears and decided that her project would be to find these a new home, no farther than her closet, of course.

"I don't even have twenty friends," she said out loud as she moved most of the stuffed bears from her bed to their new home. Names of people she knew from school paraded through her mind, but she dismissed most of them as anyone who Bella would think to invite. "Luke, James, and Ryan don't particularly count as friends since they are technically neighbors." They were fine boys, always kind and thoughtful, but she supposed they were more Judah's friends than hers.

Often, when they were all much younger, the three brothers would ask her and Judah to play with them. Boys' ideas of play and her idea of play were usually not compatible for very long, but Judah would immediately become preoccupied with the boys, climbing trees and shooting things and whatever other sorts of things they found to do. She usually ended up wandering home, alone and disappointed.

Now that she was thirteen, however, and much too old for play of any sort, she may not mind spending time with the boys—especially James, who was just a few months older than herself and terribly handsome. *We'll see,* she thought while a grin caused the edges of her mouth to turn up. Her mind slowed down and simmered with thoughts of James.

Who else might be coming? she wondered. The parade of possibilities continued marching. Jayda, Kaitlyn, Kennedy, and Mackenzie were in her class at school, and once in a while, she ate lunch at the same table. But for the most part, she did not. They seemed nice enough and had invited her to join them more often than she did, so she supposed it was alright that they were coming to her party.

For most of Jennifer's young life, she, unlike Judah, didn't seem to fit anywhere. People liked her and she wasn't exactly shy, but for reasons she didn't understand, she never really belonged. After all, she saw things in the air and heard voices that she was pretty sure nobody else did. If those girls at school ever found out … well … they could never find out. Since her parents' accident … the one that made no sense and could not be explained by anyone … the voices and faces and shadows appeared more frequently and were much crueler and condescending. Yes, these were secrets she had no choice but keep. Jennifer forced her mind away from those things and back to the party.

Of course, she expected to see her cousin, Jerrod, who was also thirteen. She and Judah had just spent the afternoon with him last week when they had no school. They didn't attend the same school, so it was always fun when they could get together. They'd spent much time together as younger kids and especially since her parents' accident.

"Mamma and Daddy," she sighed, in a bit of a panic.

For the first time since waking up this morning, she thought of her parents and realized with sadness that she didn't seem to think of them nearly as much as she used to. Jennifer scooped up her red blanket and went to the dresser where she picked up a picture of her parents. She looked at the photo for a long while before doing anything else. "I'm a teenager now, Mamma," she said sweetly and ran her finger over her mother's face in the picture. "It's my birthday today, Daddy," the girl added.

"I wish you were coming to my party," she sighed, but even as the words left her mouth, Jennifer knew that if they were here, it would have been them throwing her and Judah the party, and Bella would have been the guest.

She was torn between thinking of her party and thinking of her parents and for another moment, she stood and gazed at the old picture … one of her favorites. Her dresser was filled with pictures. Most had herself, Judah, Mamma, and Daddy, but some had just her and Mamma or her and Daddy. But this one, this one with just her parents, was her favorite.

Something startled her about the picture for a second, causing her fingers nearly to let it slip to the floor. As she stared at it, the dark eyes that were hiding behind her own were reflecting off of the glass in the frame. They, too, were looking at the picture. She could see them peering through her own eyes. Fear struck her now, as she saw evil in the reflection and wondered if it was her own, or if it belonged to another that she caught only glimpses of now and then. Jennifer shook her head violently, determined to let nothing ruin this day. Nevertheless, she became panicky about this uninvited guest that had moved in just behind her eyes. Jennifer was no longer sure that it was something altogether separate from herself. "Another secret to be kept," she whined to the photo still in her hands.

Hugging the picture as she'd done a million times before, Jennifer set it back down and turned to find Bella. She wondered if it would be wise to mention this mind-dweller to her auntie and decided, for now, to keep it to herself. She'd seen it before, although rarely. Today, now that she was thirteen, the intruder seemed to linger. No matter what she looked at, the mind-dweller became curious and would not look away. Maybe if she ignored it, gave the intruder no attention at all, it would go back to sleep and give her a reprieve from its staring eyes.

Jennifer forced her thoughts away from the intruder and back to the party, wondering what she might wear. Bella would be able to help her with such a dilemma. Jennifer had always thought that her auntie had the most beautiful clothes and couldn't wait to be big enough to borrow them. Unfortunately, today was not that day. She'd have to find something from her pile of secondhand clothes that would be suitable. Jennifer had never really cared about her clothes and it hadn't bothered her much that they didn't have the money to buy new things. But today, Jennifer thought it would be nice to have something new and beautiful to choose from. Nevertheless, she didn't have, so she would have to pick from the secondhand clothes she did have. *Good luck with that*, she thought to herself. Jennifer stepped into the hallway and shouted for her auntie.

"Bella," she called. No reply.

"BELLAAA." She waited a minute, listening, but again heard no response.

"Oh, good grief," she muttered and turned to traipse down the hallway in search of her aunt. Jennifer moved toward the kitchen, but there was no sign of Bella. She hollered her name a couple more times, neither expecting nor waiting for a response.

"Maybe she went somewhere," Jennifer thought as she headed to look out the window, but even as she said the words, she knew Bella would never leave without telling the twins that she was going. "Nope, no tracks in the driveway," she said. "Hmm, that's odd." Jennifer grabbed a few strands of her long hair and began twisting them up in her fingers, something she did when she was bored, or tired, or frustrated … which was her feeling at the present moment.

Judah also seemed to be missing. He was usually loud; banging things around or dribbling his basketball or shooting his pellet gun at a makeshift target in the basement. But now? Jennifer listened at the top of the stairs and heard nothing. She was beginning to feel a little nervous and eerily alone.

Standing in the middle of the kitchen looking around and listening for noises that would indicate where either Judah or Bella might be, Jennifer noticed that breakfast had been cleaned up and the kitchen was spotless! She also noticed that some bags of treats had been set out on the counter. Ketchup chips, pretzels, microwave popcorn, rice crispy cake with colored sprinkles, the biggest bag of salt water taffy she'd ever seen, and a gigantic red plastic tub full of cans of soda and water, all sat neatly on the cupboard. The sight caused Jennifer's excitement to stir and again she called for Bella, even though looking at the treats nearly made her forget why she was looking for her auntie in the first place.

"I'm downstairs, J," came the muffled voice.

Jennifer went running down the stairs and nearly collided with Bella, who by now was coming up the stairs. Both girls screamed and began laughing.

"What are you doing down here?" Jennifer asked.

"I was in the storage closet digging out some of Molly's fancy party things … trays and linens … oh, and her favorite tablecloth." Bella held up her arms, filled with the very things she'd just listed off, plus a few more unmentioned things.

"Oh," was all Jennifer could say. She was never quite certain how she felt when Bella would decide to use Mamma's things. After the accident, Bella and Jennifer had wrapped up many of Molly's favorite things in big blue rubber bins for safe keeping and stacked them in the storage closet in the basement.

Now, looking back, Jennifer wasn't sure why they'd decided to do that and wondered if the time had come to dig some of them out and use them again. She decided that she was glad Bella had done just that and even wondered, maybe, if they began to use some of Mamma's favorite things that it might make her feel more alive, as though part of her was still here, at the party.

"Can I help?" Jennifer asked. She picked up the tea-colored linen tablecloth that her mamma used to bring out for special occasions or Sunday dinners when they'd have company over. Jennifer carefully spread it over the kitchen table, but before she had a chance to wipe out all the wrinkles, Bella interrupted.

"That's going on the dining room table, please."

"Oh. OK," Jennifer said, pulling it off of the kitchen table and starting toward the dining room.

"J," Bella called from the kitchen, where she was wiping off a stack of serving trays and unwrapping the chocolate brown linens.

Jennifer peeked her head back into the kitchen. "What?"

"Don't you think you should get yourself ready? Your guests should be arriving in less than an hour." Bella pointed to the clock, still tick-tocking loudly from its place on the wall. "I told Judah to come up as well." Jennifer realized that when she had stopped waiting for time to pass, it had passed quickly, and as she looked up at the clock it now told her it was after 4:00.

"Oh ya!" she squealed, suddenly remembering why she was on the hunt for Bella in the first place. "That's why I was looking for you. I don't know what I should wear." Jennifer wiped her hand across the tablecloth one last time as she walked to the kitchen. "Can you help me pick something out?"

Bella held her finger up as if to shush Jennifer, and instead of walking toward the hallway that would lead to Jennifer's room, she turned the other way and headed to the front closet. Jennifer did shush but was significantly annoyed at Bella's response to her simple request for help. Her annoyance evaporated as Bella pulled a shopping bag from Finnigans out of the closet. Her eyes grew large as Bella held the bag out.

"OK, here's my help." She smiled an extra large smile as Jennifer took the bag. "I was going to wrap it, but I suppose you'd rather not be bothered." Jennifer didn't even hear Bella's words because the birthday girl loved Finnigans but had never been able to have anything from the expensive shop before.

It took only a second for the birthday girl to turn the bag upside down and let the contents tumble onto the table. The bag slid to the floor as Jennifer's hands picked up the most spectacular red jeans and a thick white belt. She held them up to herself and shifted around a little, admiring them greatly. She laid them down on the table and picked up another piece; a long-sleeved plaid button-down shirt, and finally a denim jacket.

They were perfect!

Every piece was absolutely magnificent. She'd been looking at these exact things just weeks before.

"How did you know I was looking at these?" she turned and asked Bella, not even trying to hide her surprise and overwhelming delight.

"Oh, silly Jennifer, I'm your auntie," Bella said with a smirk. "Aunties know these things."

Now with only a half hour left before the guests were to arrive, Jennifer gathered up all the pieces but set them right back down again. She skipped over to Bella and gave her a tight hug.

"Thank you, Bella. Thank you."

"OK! You're welcome. Now go put them on and do something wonderful with your hair." Bella grinned and hollered out for Judah to get himself to the kitchen ... "Pronto!"

"Judah, hurry up. I have something for you," she hollered down the stairs. Jennifer noticed Bella head back toward the front closet and decided she must have a bag of new clothes hidden in there for her brother as well.

I hope they're not matching. I hate when we match, she thought as she wandered down the hallway, clutching her new clothes.

Jennifer had nearly reached her door when she heard Bella call to her. "Oh and J, happy birthday ..."

Jennifer smiled to herself and disappeared into her room, not even hesitating as she closed the door behind her. Yes, thirteen was going to be marvelous.

Surprise at Sunset

Jennifer had not been in her room long before Bella heard a ruckus and some yelling coming from behind the door. "What could be the problem now?" Bella sighed. She rolled her eyes, even though nobody was there to see it, wiped her hands on a towel, and sauntered down the hall. She would have hurried except she knew Jennifer well, and the noise that was coming from her niece's room right now was not one of Shailmas, or black mists, or little green jars spewing fire. It was more of a thirteen-year-old annoyance blown out of proportion kind of noise.

Bella was absolutely correct in her assumptions; when she knocked on the door, surprised to see it closed, she heard a voice on the other side mumbling and griping. "What is the matter with you?! Ugh, stupid hair!"

Bella wasn't sure how to proceed, since the door was closed for the first time since she could remember. She put her hand on the knob but instead of turning it, knocked quietly (with a bit of a chuckle) and said, "May I come in?"

"OF COURSE, you should come in!" Jennifer snapped as though it were a ridiculous question. Bella tried to force her face into a solemn and concerned look, but as she turned the knob and pushed the door open, what she saw made her laugh harder. Bella immediately noticed that the problem—or at least what she was sure must be the problem—was what was going on with Jennifer's hair.

Now, Jennifer had long, dark—nearly black—hair, and she had never shown much interest in doing anything with it. In fact, Jennifer had never shown much interest in anything girlish before, so now that she had decided to do something with her hair, it was not going well at all.

"What were you trying to do here?" Bella asked, failing miserably at hiding her snickering.

"It's not funny," Jennifer whined. "I was trying to do something different, but I don't know how and I guess today isn't the day to start learning," Jennifer huffed, frustrated.

"Let me help you." Bella picked up the brush that Jennifer had thrown across the room and began working on the terrible knots the poor girl had somehow managed to twist into her hair, and untangling the elastic. "You wanted it up?" Bella asked, now a bit less entertained and a lot more helpful.

"I miss Mamma," Jennifer sighed and all of a sudden, Bella filled with compassion for this girl who should've had her mother here helping her with such things. Bella herself often became so overwhelmed with loneliness for her big sister that she sometimes forgot to consider how Jennifer must feel with her mother not here on days such as today, helping her with her hair and picking out new outfits for her birthday party. Her mamma should have been here.

"I'm sorry, J," Bella said and leaned down to hug the girl, still very tiny but as always, naturally beautiful—even with her horribly knotted up hair. "You look just like her, you know," Bella said, hoping to cheer up the moment a smidgen.

"Ya," was the only response uttered. Then a few seconds later, "I was trying to do my hair like Mamma used to do hers; you remember, up in that twisty thing." Jennifer's hands were flying around in the air as she was explaining the picture that was in her head of Mamma. "The night of the accident I sat on the bed and watched her do her hair like that." Then she became quiet, as she always did when any talk of Molly was done.

Molly was a beautiful woman, and Jennifer was looking more like her every day. They both had dark hair which beautifully highlighted their ivory skin; a few freckles dotted their noses. Jennifer and Bella could have easily spent a long while recalling memories and telling stories about both Molly and Theo, but the clock's pounding tick-tock from the kitchen reminded them that they would have to do their remembering another time.

"Let's see what we can do here … we should probably get doing it quickly." Bella finally had all the knots out and was now brushing through the long strands, gathering them all in her hand. After a couple flips of her fingers, Bella held her hand out for some pins. Within a few minutes, every hair had been secured into place.

"How's that?" Bella asked, quite proud of herself.

Jennifer looked in the mirror, turning her head this way and that, and it looked to Bella like she was satisfied.

Confident she'd made Jennifer happy, Bella headed to the kitchen to finish up a few last minute things. She was more than a little annoyed when she heard Jennifer snarl.

"Nope; that's dreadful."

Bella turned to reassure her that it was fabulous, but as she did, Jennifer reached up and pulled the pins out, her hair falling and spiraling down her back just the way it had been before.

"I looked like an old lady," she said, slamming the pins back onto the dresser. Bella decided that Jennifer was acting very much her age and decided to let her annoyance fade; there's no reason to choose frustration when humor will do.

"… and it begins." Bella chuckled, shook her head, and stepped through the door, gently closing it behind her.

"What begins?" Jennifer yelled through the closed door. She didn't expect a response and was perfectly satisfied when none came. She heard Bella hurrying Judah to get himself dressed and listened to them horseplay in the hallway. Jennifer sat for a bit and stared into the mirror, daydreaming. She tried to think of someone else she might know who was living without parents and could come up with nobody.

"It's so unfair," she whined to her reflection. "I'm only thirteen. I need my parents." Jennifer thought a pity-party might do her some good and started in on a doozy.

"I do look so much like you, Mamma," she said but wasn't sure if that was a good thing or not a good thing. Molly was indeed a beauty, so Jennifer figured she would grow up to be beautiful as well. However, she was saddened by the thought because every time she would see her reflection, she'd be reminded of her mamma. "Looking so much like someone else," she reasoned with her reflection, "robs you of being yourself." Even though she was a twin, she and Judah looked nothing alike and they had agreed many times that they were perfectly satisfied with that.

Jennifer's pity-party was interrupted by a delightful sound. *Ding Dong, Ding Dong, Ding Dong,* chimed the doorbell. With a quick kiss blown toward the pictures on her dresser, the scraggly-haired girl opened her door. A deep breath in, a giant step out, and she was on her way to what would prove to be a most splendid evening. As she stepped into the hallway, Judah did the same. He looked smashingly handsome in his new faded jeans and blue t-shirt, but she was certainly not going to tell him so. Instead, she quietly whispered her favorite greeting to her brother.

"Nerd." To which he replied straightaway his favorite response.

"Dork." They both laughed.

Halfway down the hall, they heard familiar voices of the neighbor boys. Luke, Ryan, and James had arrived, each carrying some sloppily wrapped gifts. "Mom says happy birthday to you guys," Ryan shouted as he caught sight of the twins.

The three had barely removed their coats when the bell bellowed out again. The door popped open and in came Liza, Laura, and Leslie, three of the most beautiful girls Jennifer knew. They were from her elementary school two years ago. Although Jennifer had only seen them a few times since changing schools and hadn't thought about them much, she was glad that Bella had remembered to invite them.

As friends continued appearing at the front door, some hers and some Judah's, Jennifer felt very grown up and rather important in her new clothes. She was so used to having old raggedy things that she nearly felt guilty for wearing these brand new things—especially since she knew they had been very expensive and Bella did not have much money.

Neither Judah nor Jennifer had ever minded having the old things and had grown rather fond of them, sometimes even preferring them. This was not one of those times, however, and she strutted around as proud as could be in her new clothes. *I wish I'd have left my hair up,* Jennifer thought as she noticed that Leslie's hair was almost the same as Jennifer's had been ... before she'd pulled the pins out.

Too late now, she thought, and grabbed a handful of popcorn. It surprised Jennifer how quickly everyone started chatting about nothing at all. Many of the birthday guests had gone to the same school as Jennifer the year previous, but she was shy and expected to feel nervous and awkward. She was satisfied to find she was neither of those things—at least not for long. Judah was his usual quiet self so he was no help to her. The girls, who went to a different school this year, asked Jennifer a thousand questions and gave her no time for any of the answers. Liza, who was not shy at all and was especially funny, had them all laughing in no time. Jennifer though, while she laughed and played the part she was expected to play, knew she was nothing like any of the others. She was perfectly aware, even while she giggled, of the eyes that stared through her own ... and her Shailma ... and a hundred other things that nobody else knew anything about. It separated her somehow; she wished it didn't.

The doorbell's chime echoed through the house again and as it swung open, the girls—who Bella had mentioned earlier this morning—hurried inside. Right behind them were some of Judah's friends with whom he played football. As they came in, looking so much more grown up than Jennifer felt, she decided that she would try harder to be part of their group at school.

The gift stack was growing large and Jennifer was curious to find out what kinds of things were in the boxes and bags. She hated surprises, so her curiosity about such things was overwhelming. If she could get a peek, that would be good enough for now. She was curious as well, to see who might walk through the door next. Bella had said twenty people were coming, but now that seventeen had already arrived, she wondered if perhaps she, Judah, and Bella were numbers eighteen, nineteen, and twenty. Jennifer couldn't think of any other possibilities of who would be coming, except maybe Jerrod.

All of the awkward guests squished into the living room like sardines in a can. Their plates were stacked high with chips, popcorn, and sweets, and they all chattered loudly. The boys, trying to be noticed by the girls, didn't seem to have much to say but instead threw pieces of popcorn and tried to be tough in front of the girls. Jennifer wondered if this was what Bella meant by not needing to have much of a plan for the party.

Without the doorbell chirping again and not at all surprising to Jennifer, Jerrod, and his older sister Gabby appeared in the living room.

"Hey," Jerrod said shyly.

"Happy Birthday, Jennifer," Gabby squealed and gave Jennifer a big hug. "Happy birthday, Judah," she said and kissed his cheek, making him turn red. Gabby was more Bella's age, and she moved to the kitchen to chat with her. Jennifer could hear the two whispering about something and trying to stifle their giggles. Her curiosity rose to a whole other level. Jennifer hated not knowing what was going on and these surprises were getting on her nerves.

So there must be one more coming, Jennifer thought. She ran through lists of possibilities but couldn't think of anyone who might still be coming. She became so preoccupied with her curiosity that she had, without meaning to, tuned out the conversations in the room. A piece of popcorn landed on her knee and without even thinking about it, she picked it up and instead of throwing it back like the others were doing, popped it into her mouth and gobbled it right down. Everyone laughed and began teasing her, but she was too preoccupied to notice.

Jennifer was instantly brought back to the present as the doorbell rang one last time. Jennifer looked toward the door, waiting for it to burst open like every other time, but the burst did not come. Instead, there was a loud *Rap, Rap, Rap,* on the door. She looked at Bella, who only raised her eyebrows and looked right back at her niece. After the second knock on the door, Bella finally said, "Jennifer, can you get that please?"

Jennifer was so taken by nervous curiosity, that she wasn't sure she wanted to open the door. What if it was someone she didn't want it to be? Bella was acting very strange all of a sudden, and it put Jennifer on edge. Even Judah seemed disinterested in who was on the other side of the door.

A bit apprehensive, she did get up and move toward the door, letting curiosity win out. She put her hand on the knob, turned, and pulled the door open. Her eyes instantly grew to double their size as the most wonderfully handsome young man in the entire world reached down and gave Jennifer the biggest hug any young girl could ever dream of.

He leaned down and kissed her sweetly on the forehead.

"Happy Birthday, Jennifer."

A Mind's Tangled Mess

"M.. Matt," she stuttered. It took a few seconds for her mind to grasp who was standing at her door.

"MATT!" she squealed again, so loudly that the sounds of silliness wafting from the living room stopped instantly. They all looked around, straining their necks—and their eyes—toward the doorway to see who Matt was, and why Jennifer was suddenly stumbling over her words and talking so loudly in a high-pitched voice.

Matt nodded toward the inquisitive eyes peering from the living room before putting his hand on Jennifer's shoulder and smiling his golden smile.

"I heard it was your and Judah's birthdays, and I asked Bella if I could come to your party." Jennifer blinked and stared. Her tongue stuck to the roof of her mouth. "Happy birthday," he said again and handed her a small blue box tied with a delicate white ribbon.

Stunned, she couldn't answer him. She could not take the gift from Matt. Jennifer just stood there, unable to make her thoughts get into any sensible order. She was grateful that Gabby and Bella both noticed and came to her rescue—without embarrassing her.

"Thanks for coming all this way, Matt," Bella said. She took the little blue box from him and leaned down to put her lips close to Jennifer's ear. "Surprise, J. Isn't he marvelous?" Bella giggled and set the little blue box in Jennifer's hands.

"Now, where is that brother of yours?" Matt asked, moving passed the girls.

Judah finally came to the door and stuck his hand out. "Matt, I didn't expect to see you here," he said, obviously satisfied with the surprise. Matt shook his hand and pulled him in close for a rather big-brotherly sort of hug.

"Happy birthday, Judah," he said. "I brought you a little something." Matt again dug into his pocket and pulled out a red bag tied at the top with a black string. He handed it to Judah who just looked at Bella.

"Hold onto it for now, Judah, or set it in the kitchen, maybe." She held her hand out, and he handed her the soft, red bag.

"We'll save these gifts for a bit later," Bella said with a wink. It was obvious that Bella knew something about the gifts that the others did not.

"I ... I didn't expect you," Jennifer mumbled, trying hard to keep her awkwardness hidden and sound grown up. It seemed she was so surprised that it was keeping her tongue from forming any sensible words. The poor girl just gawked and jibber-jabbered about silliness. There was probably a couple of reasons for her sudden awkwardness, the most obvious being that Matt was so very handsome ... he probably made girls nervous all the time. He and Jennifer had only known each other in Trilleah, a land of ugly cloaks and death-colored boots. They were nearly always hidden away under hooded cloaks, and nobody spent much time worrying about how they looked to the other Travelers in the dark land. When the cloaks were off their hair was usually disheveled, but they looked equally ragged, so none of them gave it much thought. But here in her kitchen, such things were not so. His handsomeness, complete with perfect hair and brilliant smile, now stood only inches away from Jennifer, making her feel outrageously awkward and childish.

She suddenly felt so small and very young now that she saw how grown up Matt was. Even so, she felt an overwhelming sense of importance that he would travel all this way to their little yellow house on 128 Viewmont Lane for her birthday. Of course, she had no idea where he lived and wondered if, perhaps, it wasn't so far away after all, and she'd just not considered it before. She certainly considered it now.

What nobody else knew, however, and what was adding greatly to her sudden nervousness, was how seeing Matt reminded her of Trilleah. Watching him here in her kitchen, happily chatting with the other guests, made her insides wretched and fearful. Oh, how her belly churned with the dark dread of returning to Trilleah.

As suddenly as her belly began to twist, the gray eyes that she'd managed to ignore for quite some time this afternoon, returned with a vengeance and peered angrily through her own. For a moment, much too long of a moment to be sure, the room darkened, and she saw countless unnamed figures spread throughout the air. She didn't realize that these beings were what the gray eyes were looking at; she'd know soon enough.

Jennifer froze for a time and could say nothing. As suddenly as the eyes appeared, they left. Her stomach turned yet again, and she had to hold her breath to keep from throwing up.

"Excuse me," she mumbled and hurried toward the bathroom. Jennifer felt as though she'd been picked up and viciously shaken, causing all her thoughts and feelings to become a tangled mess. While the excitement of her party, the gifts, and especially the small blue box Matt had given her, lingered, it all become entangled with the gray eyes that continued to stare just behind her own; back and forth the eyes came and went as they pleased. With a numbing shock, she realized that what she'd just seen—those creatures that were hanging in the air—were seen through the stranger's eyes and not her own.

Somehow, and certainly nothing she'd done in her own power, her eyes and the gray eyes had become momentarily confused, allowing each to see through the other's. Overwhelming feelings of dread stirred with knowing that Trilleah's next visit was right around the corner. She couldn't choose to not go, however, because it was Mamma who needed her there. She would do anything to free Mamma … ANYTHING!

Seeing Matt had annoyed the gray eyes and instantly reminded her of the upcoming journey and exactly what the day on the calendar truly represented. Not only was it she and Judah's birthdays and the anniversary of her parents' accident, but it also meant that Winter Solstice was tomorrow. She was not prepared; not even close.

"Oh, Mamma," she sulked to her reflection in the bathroom mirror before wandering back to the living room—her stomach only a teeny bit calmer. Would Simeon come for her? The seasons rushed by too quickly now that such a heavy time marker had come into her life. Every six months, on the days of Solstice, the gates to Trilleah opened up. She'd most likely be traveling through those gates again tomorrow—whether she wanted to or not—and she most certainly did not want to. Jennifer had never been asked to go, she just went.

Trilleah had been calling to her recently, but she'd been reasonably successful in putting it out of her mind, except for the dark presence that seemed to cover her like skin. She had become so used to it being there that she'd learned to ignore it. The eyes, though, they were impossible to ignore. The eyes often changed how she viewed her surroundings. Oh, she tried to ignore them alright, but the eyes were transforming her from the inside, forcing her to see things she didn't want to see.

But now? Now with one of the Travelers from Trilleah standing in her kitchen, the Winter Solstice had been pulled to the front and center of her mind. It shoved its way past any birthday excitement, past the pride of her new clothes, past the anticipation of all the wonderful gifts on the table with her name on them, and even past Matt's presence.

Shake it off, she told herself. She did not realize that as she thought the thought, her head literally did shake.

"What are you doing?" Jerrod asked.

"What?" she replied, acting as though her thoughts had been on the party and the guests the entire time. "What do you mean?

I'm just getting more food." She headed toward the kitchen where the food was, but also where she might get another moment or two to herself to try and get her mind off of tomorrow and back on today. She needed to focus on today, not tomorrow.

"Don't eat too much more," Bella said as she followed her into the kitchen. "The pizza will be here in a couple of minutes. So … what do you think, J?" Bella asked, grinning and glancing in Matt's direction. "You were so surprised! There's not any better birthday gift than Matt showing up, huh?" Bella was so proud of herself and while Jennifer didn't want to appear too excited about it, she couldn't hold back the corners of her mouth from turning up. She looked down at the floor to keep Bella from noticing the bright red color that was spreading over her face. She could feel it heating up.

"What's that I see, J," Bella teased. "Are you finally going to let a smile climb onto that sour puss?" That was it. Jennifer looked up, and the enormous smile that had been hiding beneath the surface let loose and splashed across her face.

She leaned in close to Bella and Gabby and whispered, "He's marvelous, isn't he?" All three girls giggled and glanced at the handsome young man.

Not long after Matt's surprising entrance, the pizza arrived. Everyone was munching down cheese, pepperoni, mushrooms, and sausage. Jennifer had carefully put the little blue box from Matt inside of her pocket, and every now and again she'd slip her hand inside to feel the smooth edges and the satin ribbon. She tried to imagine all the possibilities of what might be inside.

As they sat squished around the dining room table stuffing themselves with pizza and pop, tossing food around, and throwing their heads back laughing about absolutely everything, Jennifer's heart was being split into so many pieces that she felt dizzy going back and forth between them all. Her Mamma's beautiful tablecloth had pizza sauce and crumbs all over it. Matt was here beside her eating pizza from her favorite pizza place. Something completely unseen had enveloped her from the outside ... closer than her skin; something very much seen, had taken up residence on her insides ... just behind her eyes.

Everything was crashing in on her and she wondered if she'd be able to navigate this day much longer. Trilleah was coming tomorrow, but today she was determined to enjoy the day—no matter what may be lingering. Jennifer suddenly missed her mamma and daddy tremendously. Thankfully, her thoughts were interrupted by a horribly off-key version of "Happy Birthday." It was so bad that Jennifer could not help but burst out laughing.

"That was terrible," Judah shouted, still laughing as Bella set a big, red-velvet, chocolate birthday cake in front of the twins. Before making any wishes or blowing out any candles, Judah dragged his finger across the side of the cake, swiping a large glob of icing and popping it into his mouth.

"Mmmmm," he said, looking around the table. His sister slapped him on the shoulder.

"Judah!" she hollered.

"Make a wish," the girls chirped.

"Blow out the candles," the boys bellowed.

Hmm. A wish. The obvious wish was the one they'd wished a thousand times. A wish they'd likely continue to make for as long as they believed in wishes and perhaps, even long after that.

Jennifer closed her eyes tightly and thought, *I wish Mamma and Daddy were here.* She opened her eyes, sucked in the biggest breath she could hold, and took as long as she could to blow it out, moving her head one way and then back the other over the candles. One by one, the flames were snuffed out and replaced by tiny billows of smoke as her breath caught them. The candles that she had missed, Judah was sure to get with his hot, smelly breath.

On and on and on the party went. Food was thrown and spilled and smooshed and enjoyed. Gifts were opened ... all but Matt's, which remained set off to the side. Silly games were played and memories were made. Then, long after the sun had gone to sleep and the moon found its place in the starless sky, the guests left.

Just like that, the party was over ... and it had been marvelous.

Trinkets & Treasures

chapter five

Only Judah and Jennifer, Gabby and Bella, Jerrod, and, of course, Matt, remained. With most of the mess cleaned up—or at least piled into the kitchen and out of sight—they were all in the living room sipping on cider or hot cocoa.

"You haven't opened the gifts I gave you," Matt said.

"Oh ya!" Judah squealed, jumping up to get the red bag from the kitchen.

"I was saving it for last," Jennifer said, becoming shy all over again. She pulled the blue box out of her pocket and carefully untied the dainty ribbon. She popped open one end of the paper and gently slid the box out, letting it fall into her hand. She lifted the lid, becoming nervous for some reason that she found to be silly but nevertheless quite out of her control.

Her eyes sparkled as they saw what was inside the box. "It's beautiful," Jennifer whispered as she picked up a silver, heart-shaped locket.

"Open it," Bella said, as though she already knew what was hidden inside.

Jennifer fumbled to open it; not because it was small because it wasn't, and not because she didn't know how to because she did, but because she was nervous with everyone staring at her. After a few hushed moments, she finally managed to unlatch the locket and let it fall open in her hand.

As her eyes took in the most beautiful picture of her mamma and daddy—one she'd not seen before—Jennifer drew in her breath and felt her eyes cloud over with emotion. On one side of the locket were her parents and on the other side was a picture of Judah and herself. For a moment she lost track of the room and forgot about the people sitting there watching her.

After a few seconds, Matt spoke.

"Jennifer, when you open the locket you can look and dream and remember your parents. They are separated from you because you and Judah are on the other side of the locket. However, when you close the locket, you are together—connected by the heart. I hope you like it," he continued. "It was Bella's idea. She sent me the pictures a while ago."

"I love it, Matt, thank you," Jennifer said softly, slipping the locket over her head and squeezing it tightly. Matt didn't respond but instead tipped his head toward Jennifer and winked. For a second, Jennifer thought he might have had a small tear in his eye, but she couldn't be certain; he rubbed his eye too quickly for her to ever know.

"Open yours, Judah," Bella said.

Judah was not nearly as careful with his gift as Jennifer had been with hers. He ripped the string off and tipped the bag upside down, letting a gold pocket watch spill out. He pushed the button on the top and the lid flipped open. There was a picture of Mamma and Daddy tucked inside the top. Jennifer knew he loved it; she also knew he'd not show any emotion about it.

"Bella sent me the picture," was all that Matt said.

"It's great. Thanks, Matt," was all that Judah returned. They exchanged a look, though, that said much more than their words had.

"Do you have to leave tonight?" Jennifer asked Matt.

"Oh no," he chuckled. "I came way too far to turn around and go right back." He chuckled and winked at her, but she put her head down, looking back to the locket. She didn't want Matt to see her face go flush. Jennifer felt there was something further he wanted to say, but when she'd turned her face away, he chose not to say it.

With Gabby finishing her tea and hurrying Jerrod to finish his last gulp of cocoa, she nodded toward him and held out her mug, asking him to put them both in the kitchen.

"Thanks for coming and for the book," Jennifer said to Jerrod, who took no time whatsoever to dig his coat out of the closet and get to the door.

"You're welcome," he replied. With that, Jerrod opened the door, gave a quick nod, and disappeared into the night.

Gabby bent down to give Jennifer a kiss on the forehead and whispered, "Happy birthday, princess." She mussed up Judah's hair. "Happy birthday to you too, handsome," she whispered. Then she, too, disappeared through the door and into the darkness.

So the four remained; tired, but peaceful. Jennifer, Judah, Bella, and Matt sat quietly, understanding the bond of Trilleah that bound them together. None of them wanted to go to bed, likely because they knew what tomorrow would bring. It seemed they were happy to sit in the quiet after such a loud and rambunctious evening. Finally, as Jennifer had to blink her eyes harder and harder to keep them open, Bella suggested a good sleep would be appropriate.

"Matt, come and I'll show you to your room," Bella said.

Jennifer thought such a statement interesting since there were only three rooms in the house. Since one belonged to her, one to Judah, and the other to Bella, Jennifer perked up enough to pay attention to where Bella was leading Matt. Judah followed them as far as his room before nodding a good night and disappearing behind his door.

Jennifer noticed that he had the pocket watch firmly in his right hand. As she paid close attention to Bella and Matt, she got up and went in the direction of her bedroom. She stuck the little blue box from Matt back into her pocket and grabbed an armload of other gifts from the dining room table. She walked into her room and at first, was puzzled. However, as Bella knocked on the half-open door and came in, the mystery sorted itself out.

"J, I'm going to stay in here tonight. I hope you don't mind, but Matt needed a room," Bella explained as she rummaged through some of the things she'd brought into the room earlier.

"Auntie Bella," Jennifer said sleepily, "I don't mind at all. In fact," she said while she moved her red blanket to one side of the bed, "I think it would be great; a perfect ending to a perfect day." She smiled a sleepy smile. "Thank you for the party—it was great."

"You're welcome," Bella replied and gave Jennifer, who was already cozied into her bed, a motherly pat on her back.

"Now, J," Bella said as she walked around and sat down on the edge of the bed. She rubbed Jennifer's warm cheek with the back of her hand. "I put off bringing this up all day and most of this evening but …" she pulled a few runaway strands of hair from the girl's tired eyes before continuing. "… but I must mention the journey to Trilleah tomorrow and remind you that Simeon will be coming for you."

"I know," Jennifer muttered from under the blanket. "Good night, Auntie," she whispered as she drifted into sleep. As she did, the gray eyes just behind her own opened wide, for it was while their host was asleep they could do the greatest damage to her world … even though she wouldn't know it for many, many days.

"Hmm," Bella said to herself since Jennifer was already sound asleep. Bella stood up but with one final thought, she leaned in and kissed the girl on the forehead. "I'm so sorry, J, it is you who we need in Trilleah more than any other. Your innocence and your ability to simply believe the unbelievable are the keys that you do not even realize you carry." With that, Bella padded down the hallway to finish cleaning up the rest of the dishes. Certainly, there would be no time in the morning for such chores.

She set a few things out on the table for them to eat tomorrow in case the Shailmas came early, leaving them no time for things like breakfast or coffee. She set the coffee pot to come on in just a few hours and wondered if there was something she was forgetting, but couldn't think of anything in particular. Bella was just about to turn and head to bed when Matt appeared in the doorway.

"Need some help?" he offered.

"I'm done, but thank you," she mumbled sleepily. It was great having you come—really. The twins could not have been more surprised. It was fun, especially watching J's reaction. Since Molly and Theo … since … since the accident … their birthdays have been rather disappointing," Bella said, fumbling with something-or-other on the counter to avoid looking at Matt. "Judah has pretended like he is fine; like nothing bothers him. Jennifer has let the pain rule her days. Especially her birthdays."

Now, maybe because it was the end of a long day or maybe because tomorrow was Winter Solstice, or even perhaps because her heart was so heavy, Bella's eyes filled with tears. It took all of her willpower to keep them from spilling over. She certainly did not wish for Matt to see her in such a fragile state, so she excused herself and moved passed him to hurry down the hallway. Matt noticed and gently grabbed her by the shoulders.

He pulled her close to himself and in the kindest voice said, "Bella, you're doing a good job with the twins. I know it must be hard to raise your sister's children because she can't." He pulled her even closer, with no ill-intention, and tried to comfort her. She'd have none of it, though, and quickly wriggled free and escaped into the hallway before letting the tears fall.

He picked up a couple of glasses from the table and set them into the sink. Turning to disappear into the hallway, Matt grabbed a handful of popcorn from the counter and a bottle of water and headed off to bed. What a wonderful day this had turned out to be. It was a good thing, too, as it may be one of the last wonderful days they'd have for a long, long time. Awaiting them in Trilleah was King Shrailzhar. He'd finally figured out where the Curse Breakers were getting into his land and he had well prepared his armies for their upcoming arrival.

For a little while, all was quiet and still inside the little yellow house. Everyone was sound asleep, but even in their slumber each was nervous as they anticipated the morning's journey.

Somewhere in the night, an owl hooted, which was very unusual since it was the middle of winter and this was a colder winter than normal. It was so cold, in fact, that any sounds one might expect to hear in the moonless sky had long ago found a warmer place to wait for the raw winter nights to pass.

Nevertheless, on this unusually frigid night, if one would have strained their ears at all, they would be able to hear the "whooo-whooo" of an owl somewhere off in the distance. Nobody in the sleepy little house on 128 Viewmont Lane heard anything at all because they had found such deep rest, and a rather good thing it was because the owl's hooting was calling out to other dark creatures of the night air—creatures that wouldn't be noticed by anyone who may be looking, and creatures that didn't care how cold the temperature outside might have been, for they were themselves, the coldest creatures of all.

Invisible to the eye but present nevertheless, two outrageously enormous beings, to whom the owl had beckoned to stand guard at 128 Viewmont Lane's front entrance, appeared with all the weapons and evil intentions one might expect. King Shrailzhar had not only figured out where the Curse Breakers were entering Trilleah but also how they were traveling to his land. The king had been alerted to the Shailmas and had decided to send his biggest Nakah Warriors to stand guard at the house to keep the Shailmas out.

The king had decided that if the Shailmas couldn't get to where the Curse Breakers were waiting, they would be unable to retrieve them and therefore, have no reason to return to Trilleah.

The king was wrong ... quite wrong indeed.

Masks We Wear

chapter six

While the Travelers all had Shailmas, the king himself, of course, did not. He didn't know much about them—nothing at all really—and he most certainly did not know how to stop them. What the king was altogether unaware of was that the Shailmas did not need to gain entrance into the house because they were already in the house.

The Shailmas were always with their humans, no matter where they were. However, to get Bella, Matt, and the twins to

Trilleah, the Shailmas would need to get *out* of the house and travel the great distance in a very short time. There were no extra minutes to be battling Nakah Warriors on the journey to the dark land; not today. Even though the natural eye would never be able to see the Shailmas, their mortals, the Nakah Warriors, or anything to do with Trilleah, none of the air dwellers had natural eyes. They saw everything with their spirit eyes—those eyes that saw everything in every dimension at all times.

The very instant the Shailmas would exit the house, Nakah Warriors would spot them in the unseen realm and be after them like fury. Fortunately, the Shailmas were aware of the enormous beings who had been summoned to stand guard at the house gate. Furthermore, the Shailmas knew they would have to do battle and defeat the Nakahs ... even if the victory was only temporary.

The battle strategy for this particular Solstice journey would be simple. Because the Nakahs, who were standing guard, did not realize the Shailmas were already inside, Simeon would call for a great number of other Shailmas to come and distract the beasts, creating a diversion. One thousand Warring Shamar Shailmas would come and pretend to try and gain access to the house, which the beasts would be expecting and watching for. They would not, however, be expecting an entire legion of them.

While the great beasts were busy battling the thousand Shamar Shailmas, Simeon, Shura, Shemaiah, and Mishan would quietly ride on the wings of the air with their Travelers and hope to be unnoticed. If they were noticed, however, the two beasts watching for them would be unable to interfere with the Shailmas and their Travelers, because they'd be overpowered by the Shamar Shailmas who'd been called upon specifically for that purpose.

Yes; such a plan should work marvelously.

Simeon put in the request, calling one thousand Shamar Shailmas and at exactly 6:00 am, Bella began to stir as she heard Shura calling to her.

Bella, the time is now to rise. She rubbed her eyes and squinted, trying to read the clock. She didn't recall Shura ever waking her up before, so she lay still, waiting to hear him again just to make sure she hadn't been dreaming. She hoped she was—it turned out she wasn't.

Bella, we must hurry, the soft voice repeated to her mind. It was definitely Shura, so she quickly arose. As she was trying to sneak out of the room, the door squeaked. Bella turned back to see if she had disturbed Jennifer. It appeared she had since Jennifer now began to stir.

The girl—mostly hidden by the heavy blankets—let out a yawn and stretched, hitting her hand on the bedpost. "Ouch," she snapped and jerked her hand back under the blanket. She squinted and saw Bella standing in the doorway, looking at her oddly.

"What," she said and let her eyes fall closed.

"Nothing. I was just getting up. Shura called for me to come," Bella whispered, not wishing to disturb Jennifer any more than she already had. It didn't matter, however, and Jennifer's sleepy words slipped out.

"Simeon called me too," she muttered. "He said to get up straight away; he's taking me to Trilleah early."

Now, one would think that when a Shailma said to get up, that one would get up; Jennifer did not. She had sincere intentions of throwing back the blankets and putting her feet on the floor, but the clock told her it was too early, and so the despairing conflict between her body and her mind raged.

"Then you best get up, don't you think?" Bella asked. She had already grabbed the clothes she'd set out the night before and was heading down the hallway toward the bathroom. Jennifer mumbled something after her, but Bella did not wait to hear the excuses.

"Get up," she said again. Jennifer rolled over and tried her stretch again. This time, she made sure to miss the bedpost.

Bella was in the bathroom only a few minutes before heading toward the kitchen. As she passed Judah's room, she heard him shuffling around behind the closed door and thought maybe she could send him in to drag his sister from her bed. However, that would not make for a good morning for anyone and decided against it. She settled on the fact that it was not her job to argue with Jennifer and left that chore to Simeon.

When Bella stepped into the kitchen, she fully expected—as anyone might expect on such a morning as this morning—to be alone. She was not—alone that is—and jumped with a bit of a fright as she saw that Matt was up, dressed, and already pouring a cup of coffee. She had almost forgotten he was there and certainly didn't expect to see him in her kitchen at such an awful hour. Bella recalled his hug from the night before and awkwardness befell her, making her words a bit jumbled.

"Oh, Matt. I … I didn't expect anyone to be in here so early." She took the cup of coffee that he was holding out to her and tried to appear pulled together even as she felt more like falling apart.

"And I did not expect to be awake and pouring coffee at such an awful hour, so I guess we're even." He chuckled. It seemed evident that he was a morning person, even if their morning did begin while the sun slept. He didn't appear to be awkward at all, which only made Bella feel more awkward.

"Did your Shailma wake you?" Bella questioned. "Shura woke me, and I heard Judah up as well. Poor Simeon is trying to coax Jennifer from her bed but that's always a difficult job ... even for a Shailma." Now it was Bella's turn to giggle as she thought of Simeon trying to pull Jennifer up. She was glad to see it wasn't only herself that her niece became frustrated with in the mornings. Even Simeon struggled to get her out of bed.

"Yes, ma'am," Matt replied, inhaling a huge waft of the coffee from his mug. "I don't recall ever leaving at such an early hour." An odd sort of slushing sound was coming from the hall and both Matt and Bella stuck their heads around the corner and burst out laughing at the sight. Jennifer, who had pulled on some outrageous teddy bear slippers she'd gotten for her birthday, was shuffling her feet in angry protest along the floor. She had not bothered to get dressed and was dragging her tattered red blanket on the floor behind her.

From the "nearly grown" thirteen-year-old of last night to the "still a child" display of this morning, was quite a contrast. "She looks about six years old; poor thing," Matt snickered.

Bella took a gulp of coffee and half-heartedly offered an excuse in Jennifer's defense. "She's not good at mornings I'm afraid, no matter what time her morning might begin." They both stood, leaning on opposite walls and sipping their coffee, as Jennifer stumbled and fumbled her way into the kitchen. She acted as though she didn't see either of them and dragged herself straight past the onlookers.

"This is stupid," she mumbled. "This is too early to even be considered morning!" Yes, that was very much Jennifer's regular morning ritual of snarling and grumbling, without a doubt. It seemed that just because Matt was here, in their kitchen, Jennifer was not going to be anything but herself, even if that self was unrelentingly cranky.

She poured herself a bowl of cereal and added the milk, taking no notice—or care—that she'd slopped milk onto the floor. Instead, she heard Simeon in the belly of her mind encouraging her to eat quickly because they needed to leave soon. Furthermore, unless she wanted to enter Trilleah in her pajamas, it was in her best interest to hurry and leave time to get dressed.

"It's still dark outside Simeon … I'm tired," she mumbled out loud, which again caused both Matt and Bella to chuckle.

"Well, I must say I've never heard anyone have an argument with their Shailma before this," Matt said. "I hope he wins, but Jennifer might just go back to bed." They thought about how amusing, yet at the same time how very sad this would be, and decided that since Jennifer's presence was necessary for success in Trilleah, they would help Simeon and get Jennifer moving.

"Good morning, Miss Jennifer," Matt said. He had gotten his bowl of cereal by now, and as he sat down to join her at the table, leaned over and gave her a kiss on the top of her head. "How was your sleep?"

If anyone could get her going, it would be Matt. Even that, though, was doubtful. Bella waited for her response.

"Short," she huffed.

"Mine was short too, but now it's time we get to Trilleah and see who has arrived before us ... or who might be coming that hasn't been there before." He was searching his brain to find anything that might interest Jennifer and encourage her to eat a bit quicker and be a little less grouchy.

Judah appeared around the corner just then. He loved the mornings and often drove the others a bit crazy with his highly annoying state of *happy*.

"Good morning," he smirked, glancing at his sister. He plucked a handful of grapes from the bowl on the counter and tossed a few toward her. Jennifer ignored the grapes but did manage to throw a nasty glare back at her brother.

Matt kept chattering to Jennifer. "Maybe some fascinating new Travelers will be there—perhaps some charming thirteen-year-old boys," he said, poking gently at her arm.

"I doubt it," she snapped.

"Boy, she is a tough one in the mornings, huh, Judah," Matt teased. When Jennifer looked at him long enough to make sure he saw the glare she was throwing him, he winked at her. A tiny smile may have tried to curl its way onto her face, but Jennifer was very stubborn, especially in the mornings, and she chased it away immediately.

"OK," Bella interrupted. She stuck her empty bowl into the sink and bent down to wipe the milk from the floor. "Enough joking around from you, Matt. No more grapes for you, Judah, and enough antics from you, Miss Jennifer Lillian!" Bella took both their empty bowls and added them to her own in the sink and ran hot water over the pile.

"Go and get dressed, J."

Bella helped Jennifer by pulling out her chair. Jennifer attempted to make it screech by scraping it across the floor and made an amusingly outrageous spectacle of standing up, even though she was trying to be anything but amusing.

"Oh stop. You are thirteen now, and we have no time this morning for such silliness; now go quickly."

Jennifer rolled her eyes and huffed, but she did march herself down the hallway. To Bella's satisfaction, she moved a bit faster than before, but not enough to be especially beneficial.

"Well," Jennifer turned and looked back at Matt before getting too far down the hall, "here we go again." She had a sorrowful look in her eye that made it clear she did not want to go, but also a hint of desperation that said she'd do anything to free her mother's soul from the Forest of Waiting Ones. Matt pursed his lips tightly together, gave her a look of compassionate understanding, and nodded his head.

He'd always been able to bring joy to someone's heart, whether they were sad or angry or just generally grouchy. He just had a way about him that brought smiles to faces. However, he knew there was no smile hidden in Jennifer's spirit this morning because he felt the same way; heavy and doubtful and full of dread.

Here we go again, was the same thought that lingered in his own mind, which is perhaps why it was so easy for him to read the sorrow in Jennifer's eyes. If there were any other way he would take it, but he wanted to free the trapped soul of his father just as much as anyone else wanted their lost ones to be redeemed from the curse.

So, Trilleah would be the battleground on which the war would be fought. They would continue to return each Solstice until they had found every clay tablet needed, and he, though tired and afraid, would continue to smile and do his best to make everyone else feel confident, even if he wasn't. At least, that was what his father had always told him.

"Matthew," he would say in his deep, strong, fatherly voice, "No matter what comes your way in this life, always be brave, for you are never alone. Even when your insides are shaking with fear, be brave on the outside because that way you can trick your insides. Even when you are most afraid, smile and pretend and do what you must do. That is bravery, my son. Sometimes, we need to do the hard things, no matter if we are afraid or not." And then would come his father's most famous of all lines. "If you can't conquer your fear, then ignore it and conquer the problem. Leave your fear nothing to cling to."

Matt had thought of that speech hundreds of times, perhaps because his father had repeated it hundreds of times, or maybe because it had new meaning now that he spent so much time afraid. He often wondered if his father knew about Trilleah, or Malleana Forest, or maybe even King Shrailzhar, and had wanted to prepare Matt without him knowing he was being prepared for anything at all.

Even now, as Matt repeated the bravery speech again in his mind, he wondered if his father had known about the Shailmas or even if, perhaps, he had a Shailma of his own before the Trows stole his soul. Before his father was imprisoned in the Forest of Waiting Ones by the evil curse, Matt always assumed when his father had repeated the part about "never being alone" that he meant he would always be there. But now? Yes, Matt was convinced his father knew about the Shailmas.

"I wonder," he accidentally said out loud.

Sometimes when one wonders so deeply, they forget they are the only ones who know about the thoughts lingering in their minds and accidentally cross over into the place where others can hear. Judah did hear him and asked about the words.

"You wonder what?" Judah's voice startled him, and Matt came back in an instant, with a bit of a start, from all his intrusive wonderings.

"Oh, nothing," he said and quickly changed the subject. Maybe one day he would share his father's speech and ask others what their thoughts on it might be, but now was certainly not the time, for Jennifer was padding her way back toward them. Furthermore, he was not ready to let anyone know that his confidence was nothing more than a mask he wore and that he was really just doing it afraid.

Shailmas Delayed

"I'm ready anytime," Jennifer muttered, still a bit grouchy sounding but thankfully, less than before.

"Good to see," Bella replied. "Now we can wait for the Shailmas to retrieve us when *they* are ready. I'm so glad they know when it's time to leave and that we don't have to do anything in particular but be ready when they come," Bella said. Matt agreed wholeheartedly, and a new conversation about the Shailmas began as Bella poured herself another cup of coffee.

Jennifer's mind had never considered most of the questions now being raised by Matt and Bella and she listened quietly. She wondered why she, Bella, or Judah had never talked about them. The conversation quickly became a bit dull to Jennifer, and she considered grabbing the new book that Jerrod had given her for her birthday. She didn't think it was the best time to start a new book, however, because she was sure that there was little chance she'd be able to concentrate on that or anything else, for that matter. As she contemplated it, the gray eyes blinked a few times, catching Jennifer's attention.

What do you WANT? she shouted inside her mind. *Why don't you leave me alone?* The voice that had accompanied the gray eyes last night was silent now, making Jennifer that much more agitated. She could see them, though ... peering at her from the inside. At least, Jennifer thought they were looking at her.

What she could not possibly have understood, even if someone would have explained it to her, was that the eyes were not looking AT her. They were looking THROUGH her. She was the host that carried the gray eyes to and from Trilleah. They had latched onto her in the cursed land, of course, but Jennifer was just the one who carried them so they could see. The longer they were with her, the more they learned to hate her.

Even though the gray eyes were sent by King Shrailzhar to spy on the Travelers while they were absent from Trilleah, it was Jennifer the gray eyes had become obsessed with. It was her they were plotting against. It was their host who they needed to ruin—before she ruined them. They were quite aware of the power that Jennifer was yet unaware she carried. They knew if they didn't end her before she understood such a power, it would be too late. The eyes had tried numerous time to explain that to King Shrailzhar, but he refused to listen.

Simeon, when are you coming? she whined. Jennifer was hoping that with the presence of her Shailma, the gray eyes would leave her alone. Instantly Simeon replied, which finally caused Jennifer's face to turn upright as a smile spread across it. She always loved when he answered her quickly, for she felt as if he had finally decided that she could be the boss, which, of course, she couldn't be. Sometimes it didn't hurt to believe some things even if they weren't necessarily quite as true as you'd like them to be. This was one of those times.

The truth of the Travelers' reality would be far too hard to accept. Believing things were a certain way even though they were not, would be the one thing that may give Jennifer and the others the bravery they would need to keep going on their journey into the darkest crevices and fire-filled chasms of Trilleah … maybe.

Bella stood up and poured the last few gulps of her coffee down the drain. "I can't drink any more of this," she grumped. "I was sure we'd be in Trilleah by now. I don't understand why Shura woke me over an hour ago if he wasn't going to take me to Trilleah right away." That was enough to stir Jennifer up again, and Bella wished she'd have kept her words to herself.

"I could still be sleeping," she huffed. "This is stupid ... just sitting here waiting."

Matt and Bella just looked at one another. Bella rolled her eyes and dramatically swiped her arm across her forehead as if to faint, trying to match the drama Jennifer was displaying. Matt chuckled. Jennifer could not possibly be more theatrically grumpy this morning if she tried. She didn't intend for her production to be amusing, but it was indeed.

"She's so funny before noon," Judah announced, purposely loud enough for his sister to overhear. "I hope she never changes because I get up early just to watch her misery." He laughed to himself as he followed her into the living room, a couple of grapes in his hand.

"Leave her alone now, Judah," Bella hollered after him.

Before very long at all, the squeak from the rocking chair was louder and more annoying than usual, perhaps because it was still earlier than anyone should ever be awake. The sun hadn't even stirred yet. Perhaps it squawked louder than normal because both Matt and Bella were a bit impatient with all this waiting, or perhaps it was because when Jennifer read a book, she became so entrenched in the story that she'd rock more intensely. At least she wasn't yelling at Judah ... yet.

"Sitting around waiting is making the time go so slowly. I'm not in any hurry to go, but the Shailmas certainly seemed to be in a hurry earlier. Now, I don't see their reasons at all," Bella whined. Of course, neither she nor Matt knew that the reason for such an irritating delay was the two unseen Nakah Warriors ferociously guarding the front door. If they could have gotten even a shadowy glimpse of the beasts, they'd have run right back to their beds and pulled the covers up high, hiding their heads and shivering with fright. The Travelers would have refused to leave the house if they had any idea what was on the other side of the door. They had no understanding that they were waiting for a thousand Shamar Shailmas to come and be a distraction so they could escape unharmed. They were not yet aware that the two worlds were colliding; themselves caught in the middle.

Neither Matt nor Bella had yet learned to trust their Shailmas completely; Matt even a little less than Bella. If they had, they'd have known that something was stirring out of their sight that had caused such a delay.

"I'm going to go make the beds and do these dishes. I have to find something to do other than sit here and wait and listen to the ticking of that stupid clock." Bella stood up and stuffed the plug into the sink, squeezed some flowery smelling soap under the tap, and turned the water on.

"I can do these dishes, Bella," Matt offered. He stood and rolled up his sleeves.

"Are you sure?" Bella asked.

"I know how to do dishes," he chuckled. "Besides, that ticking clock is beginning to get on my nerves as well. It's mocking us!" He adjusted the water a tiny bit and reflected for a moment on his past. "After my dad was gone, it was just mom and us boys. Mom taught us real quick how to do chores."

Bella listened intently and realized this was the first time she'd ever heard Matt talk about his family. He was usually the one listening to the other Travelers talk about their own life's burdens because, well, he was good at listening. He would get this look in his eye that made you want to tell him things you couldn't tell other people. You just knew he was listening hard, both to the words and to the heart. It was like his eyes would transform into these pools of the bluest water and invite you to dive right in, bearing your entire soul.

So now, Bella was distracted from the waiting and she found it nice to be the listener for a change. "How many brothers do you have?" she asked, genuinely interested.

"There are six of us boys; I'm the oldest," Matt answered.

"Six!" she squealed. "No wonder your mother taught you to do chores. She sure couldn't have done it all on her own." Bella suddenly understood the desperation Matt must feel to work toward freeing his father's soul. Being the oldest, he surely must have carried a heavy burden of responsibility for his family.

Bella wanted to hear more, but she couldn't think of even one thing more to ask and he didn't offer any more information. Matt just nodded at her, shut the water off, and stuck his hands in the sink. Bella must have looked foolish just standing there, or perhaps she was making Matt feel slightly uncomfortable because he looked over his shoulder and said, "Weren't you going to make the beds?"

"Oh … um … yes, I was," she nodded and headed down the hall. As she walked past the living room, Bella stuck her head in to see what the twins were up to. She was pleasantly surprised to find both Judah and Jennifer reading books from their birthday the night before. *Maybe they are growing up a little*; she thought to herself.

When Bella came to the first bed, she just stood there looking at it, wanting more to crawl under the blankets than to straighten them. Instead, she did neither. She slumped herself onto the side of the bed and began asking Shura what was going on. She had been making these trips long enough to know that if they were delayed, there was a good reason for it. However, she did not wish to mention such a thing to the others, especially to Jennifer, and take the risk of adding unnecessary fear. If there was a reason to be more fearful than normal, Bella would carry that burden herself.

Even though it might appear that the Shailmas gave their Travelers no options in such matters, the truth was, that if any one of them had refused to go to Trilleah, their Shailma would be unable to force them. It was something each person had to choose for themselves every time the gates were opened. The last thing Bella wished to do was frighten Jennifer before they left, in case she refused to go.

So far, nobody had come to learn the reason Jennifer was the one person, in particular, who was needed to break the curse of the Trows. They had not fully decided if her presence in Trilleah was to find the last of the tablets or to break the curse or for another reason altogether, but the reason did not particularly matter. What did matter was that Jennifer continued to arrive safely to Trilleah each time the gates opened. If she ever chose to not return to the land, none of the souls would be set free from the curse; the forest would hold them forever.

Bella had fought and argued with Shura for many months to keep Jennifer from even knowing about the land, the curse, or the forest, but Shura would not relent.

She is needed more than any other—even more than you, he would repeat to her over and over and over. Finally, and with a dread-filled heart, Bella relinquished her argument and gave Shura permission to call upon Jennifer's Shailma to make his presence known to her and take her to Trilleah. Of course, Bella's permission was never really required, but she refused to believe that.

Bella regretted it every day since, but she knew the choice was never really hers to make.

No Looking Back

chapter eight

Bella realized that she had been sitting thinking for quite some time when Matt appeared in the doorway, his face covered with a cheeky grin. "What a marvelous job you did of making the beds," he teased, flicking the few drops of water from his hands toward her.

"Oh, my," Bella squealed, stood up, and grabbed the blankets. But before she could pull them up, Matt interrupted.

"No time now," he whispered and grabbed her by the hand. "My Shailma has instructed me that it's time to go—immediately—but this time will be different." She turned to look at him.

"What do you mean, different?" she asked, obviously flustered by the lack of understanding at his confusing statement.

"I'm not sure," he said, trying to keep his voice calm. "Mishan just said that we'd all be leaving together this morning and that we were to simply walk out the side door. He also warned sternly about the importance of using the SIDE door."

"That's different, alright!" Bella said, sounding even more confused and even a bit panicked.

"We need to grab the twins and get out that door immediately."

Almost before Matt had finished his last sentence, and at precisely the same moment that he led Bella into the hallway, Jennifer and Judah came running down the hallway nearly crashing into them. Matt had to let go of Bella's hand and grab onto Jennifer to keep her from knocking them all over.

"Simeon …" she blurted, huffing and puffing and trying to catch her breath. She licked her lips, took a deep breath and let it out slowly. "Simeon just spoke so clearly to my mind," she said, slower now. "He said it was urgent and very necessary that we leave through the side door … IMMEDIATELY!" She hesitated again, still breathing loudly. "He said to come and find you because we must all leave together … right now!"

She and Judah both appeared to be full of panic, as if the house was on fire.

"OK, Jennifer," Matt said, taking her small, dainty hand in one of his big ones while reaching back for Bella to grab his other hand. "Now I know why, maybe, I'm here this morning," he said. "Let's go."

Matt led them to the door at the side of the house, right off of the kitchen, and again, Matt knew the Shailmas were telling the truth because there was no way that both he and Jennifer would have thought to go out the side door and leave together if the Shailmas had not told them to do so. That had never happened before where two of the Travelers came up with such specific instructions at precisely the same time. The only explanation had to be that the Shailmas knew something the Travelers did not, and were leading them in truth and wisdom. The wise thing to do was follow the instructions exactly as they'd been given.

"I hope we can get out that door," Bella said. "It hasn't been opened since the summer."

"Don't worry about that, Bella," Matt squeezed her hand. "If the Shailmas are so concerned about us leaving through that door, they will make sure we can open it." His voice sounded confident, which was what both girls needed at the moment. If they'd have known that inside Matt was everything except confident, they would have been extraordinarily shaken and filled with dread, but Matt did not let them know—he didn't even hint about such a thing.

As the four of them scurried to the side door, Matt was repeating his father's speech about bravery—in his mind where no one else would hear.

Judah reached the door first, unlatched it, and put his hand on the knob. Jennifer laid her hands overtop his and tried to help him pull the door open. Matt noticed how very small her hands looked and his heart felt sad for such a young girl having to walk such a difficult journey.

Judah turned the knob and inhaled deeply.

Jennifer shut her eyes.

Together, they pulled on the door.

They were all surprised (even Matt, who didn't let anyone see his surprise) that the door so easily swung right open.

"OK," Matt said, sounding like the boss, and right now both Jennifer and Bella were perfectly content to let him take the role. In fact, both girls were very thankful he was here. Likely, Judah was as well, but he had become the man of the house in the last couple of years and was not about to let the girls down. Not now.

"Let's go," Matt said, directing Jennifer through the door while still leading Bella. He did not let go of either of the girls' hands just yet. "Judah, take Bella's hand," he said.

Jennifer stepped through the door and the moment her feet were both outside, she disappeared. Next, Judah stepped out, then

Bella, and finally, Matt. All were gone in the blink of an eye. It was as though they'd stepped through the air and it swallowed them up, hiding them from anything that may be looking in their direction; whatever had been watching for them had missed their departure.

Their Shailmas had been ready and waiting for their riders, and had quickly gathered them up and whisked them to Trilleah, where the king would most certainly be awaiting their arrival. Jennifer saw that Judah was close beside her. They both looked behind and could see Matt and Bella on the backs of their Shailmas —a sight neither had seen before. In fact, they could all see one another other and unlike in Trilleah or back home, they could see their Shailmas.

Jennifer, like all the Travelers, was always overwhelmed when her eyes could see the Shailmas, for indeed they were magnificent and enormous creatures. If only their eyes could always see past the atmospheric veil that almost always blocked their vision, they'd have never been afraid again, for the Shailmas ... these ones who were always with them ... were simply spectacular and tremendous and mighty. Fear could not remain with the Travelers in the visual presence of the Shailmas.

Jennifer looked past Bella and Matt, as something else altogether horrifying caught her eye. She gasped and pointed below, back to their little yellow house that was already far, far below. Standing at the front door were two most enormous beasts, and in an instant, she knew why the side door had been their portal. They would have never gotten out otherwise, not with those wild looking devilish beasts standing guard.

The beasts were not noticed by the Travelers before their Shailmas retrieved them, but now, in this mid-space flight, they could see all sorts of things not seen before now. The veil that normally hung in the air and separated them from all that dwelled unseen was, for a reason they could not understand, gone. It was yet to be determined if this was a good thing or not a good thing. None of the Travelers knew whether to close their eyes so as not to see what was dwelling among them or to keep them wide open and take in every sight they could.

Those beasts standing guard at their front door had atrocious and impenetrable armor covering them, from what Jennifer could make out; although she was quite a distance away and had to squint hard to see anything at all. Furthermore, it looked like they were holding spears—or machetes—perhaps. They looked at least twelve feet tall, but Jennifer quickly realized they must be even bigger, since the tips of the spears were the same height as the top of the house. She was having terrible trouble believing what she was seeing.

"Those are Nakah Warriors," Simeon whispered to Jennifer. "They have been sent to defeat anyone who may try to journey to Trilleah. Their purpose is to stop the Travelers before reaching the land. We outsmarted them though, for we were already aware of their presence, as we always are."

Immediately, Jennifer became afraid and dug both hands deep into the back of her Shailma.

"Stop looking back," Simeon whispered to her. "Never look back, Jennifer. You must always keep focused on what's ahead and let me worry about what's behind." While Jennifer knew, now more than ever before, to always trust Simeon, she also knew that trusting him and obeying him were two very different things. She had no trouble whatsoever trusting him, but obeying him? That was much more difficult—especially when what she had just seen stationed at their front door hung squarely in the front of her mind.

She turned one more time, and although she considered Simeon's words, she chose to disobey them and look back. The very second her eyes caught sight of the two Nakah Warriors, she wished with all her wishes that she'd listened to Simeon. She knew now that obeying him was as important as trusting him. But now it was too late.

As she turned to look back, her eyes caught the eyes of one of the beasts and that was enough. She was unable to look away soon enough and when her eyes caught the Nakah Warrior's, he alerted the other and both were speedily on their way. The two mammoth Nakah Warriors raised their weapons and pointed them at Jennifer, Judah, and the others. They were coming and Jennifer knew it was because she'd done what Simeon had told her not to do. She knew her disobedience had alerted the Nakah Warriors to the

Travelers' whereabouts and that indeed, they were all in much trouble.

"Simeon," she called out, overtaken with fear and dread. "SIMEON" she cried out again. Jennifer had so much in her heart, but no other words would come out. She laid flat on his back, wrapped her small arms around his neck, hung on as tight as she possibly could, and allowed fear to paralyze her. She tried to become as small as possible, but she knew she could never be so small as to be unseen by the Nakah Warriors. Bella noticed and so did Matt, although Judah paid no attention. They too, it seemed, had seen what was behind them and while Bella was just as panicked as Jennifer, Matt still appeared to be without any fear whatsoever.

The four of them felt as though they were trying to outrun a wildfire that was licking at the heels of their boots. It was a helpless feeling since the only thing the Travelers could do was hang on and trust their Shailmas. That trust was being pushed to its farthest limits now as the Nakahs were quickly gaining ground on them.

The Shailmas sped up, but not nearly enough to keep Jennifer calm. She looked at Judah, who was always brave, and hoped he'd give her a bit of comfort. She was disappointed, though; even Judah now looked horribly afraid.

"Is this as fast as you can go, Simeon?" Jennifer screamed. She had been hanging on so tightly that her fingers were beginning to tingle from a lack of blood flowing into them. Terrified, she loosened her grip the smallest amount she could—which was hardly any at all. Pain shot through every finger as she forced them to loosen up a little more.

"I am one of the fastest of all the Shailmas, Little One, but my speed is not the problem here. The problem here," Simeon paused for an uncomfortably long moment, "is your lack of obedience." She wanted to argue against such a heavy accusation but found she could not because, deep down in her belly, she knew he was right.

The fact was that the nightmarish Nakah Warriors were completely unaware the Travelers had left the house until she looked back the second time—after Simeon had told her not to—and she caught the darkness in their eyes with the light that glimmered from her own. Simeon had been very clear when he told her not to look back and she, in her stubborn curiosity, ignored the instructions and did precisely what she was told not to do.

Now, these savage devils, with spears pointing, were gaining quickly on them. It seemed there was little that could be done now to avoid being overtaken by them. The Travelers' only hope was in their Shailmas. Feeling dread pour into her, filled with a full measure of it by now, in fact, Jennifer called out to Judah who was close but at the same time, so very far away.

"Judah, I'm so sorry," she screeched, wanting to hold her hand out to him but far too scared to let go of Simeon.

Judah said no words and just looked back at her. His eyes stared directly into her own which brought some comfort, although only a very tiny amount. It always caught her by surprise how one look from her twin brother could bring her comfort, no matter how terrible she felt inside. It was as though he said a hundred things with just one look, without ever opening his mouth.

Unfortunately, this time the comfort was shallow and short-lived. There seemed to be no hope of escape from the oncoming Nakah Warriors and it was Jennifer's fault.

She buried her face, no longer wanting to watch or see anything that was going on around her. She wished deeply that the atmosphere would close itself back up and blind her eyes once again. She would just wait for the end to come and hope that it would come quickly.

"I'm so sorry, Mamma!" she cried.

"Please forgive me, Daddy," she whispered.

1000 Shamar Shailmas

Jennifer waited for what seemed like forever, but rather than see anything, or feel anything, she heard something. First, she heard Bella scream out … "LOOK!"

Jennifer didn't want to look because she didn't want to see what she believed was going to be the end of her. Her biggest hope now was that there were no Trows around to steal her soul and lock it away in Malleana Forest. No, Jennifer most certainly would NOT look.

She was overtaken by such an overwhelming sadness, because it seemed that she was not going to be able to finish collecting the tablets and free her mamma's soul. The sorrow was great indeed, but those miserable feelings were quickly overshadowed by the wretched realization that she would be separated from Judah as well, and that was too much for her to bear. The most horrible of all her swirling thoughts was that they might all end up trapped in the forest with no one left to break the curse.

Giant tears were filling her eyes, causing them to burn. Jennifer wanted to wipe them away with the backs of her hands, which was her regular habit, but she didn't dare let go of Simeon. Again, she heard Bella shriek.

"Jennifer … Judah … LOOK!" As Jennifer tried to work up the courage to open her eyes and see whatever it was that Bella was shouting about, her ears filled with an unimaginable sound; a deafening sound. It was the sound of a desperate howling wind when it echoes in the valleys and bounces off the mountains ... only a thousand times louder.

It was that sound that stirred her curiosity. As Bella—and now Judah and Matt—continued in her hollerings to LOOK, Jennifer forced her eyes open and lifted her face to look at Bella. Her eyes, still stinging, looked directly into the face of her auntie, expecting to see fear and dread. Instead, what she found in Bella's eyes was exactly the opposite of fear and dread. She whipped her head around to look at Judah and then Matt. She saw the same expression on all their faces—an odd excitement, which of course, stirred up Jennifer's inquisitiveness enough to overshadow her dread. She turned her head to look at whatever was giving everyone else such a peculiar excitement.

In an instant, Jennifer's eyes grew large in her effort to take in all she was seeing. She was overwhelmed and swung her head back to look at Judah, who was also trying to see everything that was going on around them. Jennifer's head went back and forth between the countless warrior beings that had come between the Travelers and the two spear-wielding Nakahs. She was trying to make some sense of the indescribable event, but she and the others were unable to make any sense of it at all.

Jennifer heard an unexpected chuckle and looked around. With nobody close enough to be able to hear them, she realized it was coming from Simeon.

"These glorious creatures you see, my dear Jennifer, are Shamar Shailmas. I called for them hours ago while you were still trying to wake up from your sleep. I beckoned them to come and battle the two Nakah Warriors who were deployed to keep you out of Trilleah today."

Jennifer heard Simeon's words and was instantly grateful for his voice. She was also grateful he was allowing her some understanding—although limited—of this unbelievable event. If she had not been in the midst of seeing it for herself, she would never have believed it, for it was truly unbelievable.

Neither Simeon nor the other Shailmas slowed down even for a moment, so it was hard to watch for too long. In the short time they could still see the battle below them, their eyes drank in the most magnificent—yet terrifying—of sights; far beyond what Jennifer's wild imagination had ever even considered.

The Shamar Shailmas, as Simeon had called them, were enormous and obviously powerful. Too many to count, they stood side by side and held their wings high, intertwining into a wall so thick the two Nakah Warriors looked small and useless; easily defeated.

There was no way the Nakahs could get through the massive wall of winged Shamar Shailmas to attack the Travelers. However, they seemed to believe they could, or at least, they were determined to break through and kept trying this way and that. If they moved up in an attempt to get over the wall of Shamars, the Shamar Shailmas would rise as a solid wall and block them thoroughly. The same thing happened if the Nakahs tried to go around or beneath. The entire army of Shamar Shailmas moved as though they had become one impenetrable being.

At one point, while the whole baffling event was still visible, the Nakah Warriors tried to trick the Shamar Shailmas. One Nakah went above while the other went beneath, but that too, proved to be useless. As they tried this daring maneuver, the countless Shamars split in half, forming two walls. From what it looked like, this was the move they had been waiting for. Perhaps they'd had this battle, or one like it, before. It seemed as though they were expecting such a silly move from the much less powerful Nakah Warriors.

If two Nakah Warriors standing together looked small in comparison to the countless Shamar Shailmas, one Nakah Warrior looked downright puny and ridiculous.

As the Nakahs came near the great walls of Shamar Shailmas, they were easily overtaken. The last thing the Travelers were able to see before they were out of sight filled them with such confidence in their safety that any fear which may have been lingering, vanished.

The Shamar Shailmas circled the individual Nakahs, knocking the spears from their grip. As they circled and came closer and closer to each other, the Shamars unified into one giant mass, easily enveloping the pathetic and powerless Nakah Warriors. The gigantic ball of Shamar Shailmas became smaller and smaller, somehow folding into itself until the whole thing was simply gone.

Jennifer, Judah, Matt, and Bella's eyes all searched this way and that for something—anything—indicating where they may have gone or if they were going to return, but they found nothing at all. Only the swirling air around them remained.

"Where did they go? Where did they take the Nakahs, Simeon?" Jennifer asked, bewildered.

"The Shamar Shailmas destroyed the beasts, Jennifer; they stopped their lives when they circled them and pulled themselves together. No evil thing can withstand the circling Shamar Shailmas; their breath was removed," was Simeon's inconceivable answer.

Jennifer supposed that he figured she would understand such a seemingly simple answer as "their breath was removed," but she didn't understand it at all. In fact, all it did was cause a thousand more questions to begin rising in her belly, but she was too amazed and altogether flabbergasted to know which to ask. One question, however, did hover above the rest, so she dared to ask it, although she was certain she didn't want the answer and confident she wouldn't understand it anyway.

"Where did the Shamars go?" She was not sure whether she'd hear an answer or not, as Simeon was always unpredictable in such things. Jennifer was surprised when he answered her straightaway.

"They went back to where they came from," was his senseless response which led, of course, to another question.

"You say Shailmas are always near. Are they near now?"

"Oh, Jennifer, my dear one, there are so many things you don't understand and so many things you do not have the ability to understand, yet you continue to search for answers." She was not sure if Simeon meant his comment to be a good one or not a good one but either way, she realized that he did not answer her question, and she contemplated whether or not to be offended by him. She decided against it and instead reworded her question.

"OK, Simeon, but are they near now?"

"Oh no, Little One, they are not," he said out loud to her. It seemed that here, in this one place somewhere between the little yellow house now out of sight, and Trilleah, only in this one place of in-between, everything was different; more real. In this portal, she could see Simeon, feel him, touch him, and have conversations —like friends would—outside of their thoughts. They could speak with their tongues and hear with their ears. Jennifer realized that she liked this place—this portal—very much. It would be in this place where she would get to know and understand many things.

Simeon continued his explanation.

"When I told you that your Shailma was always near you, that is precisely what I meant. YOUR Shailma, who, of course, is me. The Shamar Shailmas are no longer here because we no longer need them; at least not right now. They will return if we have need of them.

"Every person has a Shailma assigned to them at their birth and that Shailma is with you until your death. But the Shailmas you see here: me, Shura, Shemaiah, and Mishan, we are Seraphic Shailmas—your unseen guardians of the air, if that helps you to understand." It did not help her to understand, but she kept quiet, hoping for more information.

"However, Little One, countless types of Shailmas dwell far from here and the Shamar Shailmas are some of those. They, too, dwell in the air but are not assigned to any specific human. Rather, their assignments are quite specific, such as battling the Nakah Warriors."

Jennifer was becoming confused, and she knew she'd been given too much information already.

"OK," was all she said. He took her words to mean that she had enough information and changed the subject.

"We are almost to Trilleah, Little One."

This topic was no better than the last one, and the response showed her feelings about the entire situation. *I already want to go home, and I'm not even to Trilleah yet*, she huffed. As soon as she thought her thought, she wished she could unthink it. It is difficult, nearly impossible, really, to be so aware of your thoughts that you are able not to think them. Jennifer could not figure out how to decide whether to think or not think a particular thought, it was just there, in her mind, as though she had no control whatsoever over any of them. These kinds of things never mattered at all before Trilleah ... before Solstice ... before Simeon.

But now? Now that there was an incredibly powerful force that could know her thoughts at the same time she thought them. That idea itself made her so confused that she wished she could stop thinking altogether. She and Judah had discussed this very thing many times. Neither of them appreciated having their thoughts known, and just yesterday, Jennifer was complaining of such a burdensome intrusion. Judah, however, made an obvious point with which she had to agree.

"It seems," he had pondered out loud, "that I would much rather have Shemaiah know the unkind, unpleasant, and unhelpful thoughts I think if it means he is also going to know my desperate, 'Help Me' thoughts." He continued before Jennifer could interrupt.

"If I had to choose between my Shailma knowing all of my thoughts and knowing none of them, I would choose that he knew all of them." Judah folded his arms across his chest as if to indicate that his choice was the right one and everyone else should think likewise, and the conversation was now over.

Jennifer supposed her brother was right. However, she most certainly was not going to let him know it. "I don't know, Judah," she said instead.

"Oh, J, you are crazy and you know I'm right," he shot back. "You're just too stubborn to admit it." He'd been sitting on the kitchen counter all the while, something their mother always told him not to do, and now quite thoroughly tired of the conversation, he jumped down and headed for the basement.

She was just about to holler something annoying and bossy after him, but he beat her to it. "Just stop thinking stupid thoughts," he shouted at her as he headed down the stairs, laughing uproariously.

"I don't know what he finds so interesting down there," she said out loud, even though she was the only one left in the room. "And I don't think stupid things," she huffed after Judah, even though in her heart she knew that she often did.

Now, even as she replayed bits and pieces of their conversation from the kitchen just yesterday, she forgot that Simeon heard all of it. Part of her wished Simeon would always remind her he was there listening, but part of her thought it might make her feel crazy to be having continual conversations with a being she could not see. She already wondered if she was a bit mad, and Judah—telling her repeatedly that she was—did nothing to build her confidence.

Stupid Judah, she thought.

Two Are Better Than One

chapter ten

Simeon interrupted what was about to be a very satisfying tangent against her brother, with a quite unsatisfying speech.

"You and Judah are a perfect pair and in Trilleah, you will begin to rely on each other more than might be desired by either of you. What one does not see, the other will. What one cannot hear, the other can. You need to stay near Judah; you will need each other to escape Trilleah, Jenny.”

Such information did not make her happy or encouraged. It nearly made her lose all hope before they even reached the dark land. Nevertheless, Simeon continued.

“Where one goes astray the other will rescue, and when one is deceived the other will know the truth. Jennifer, Little One, if you fail to rely on Judah … if he fails to rely on you … neither of you will leave Trilleah at all.” And with that horrible notion now firmly rooted in her mind, Simeon became silent.

Sometimes it takes great effort to be thoroughly disgruntled, while other times it takes no effort whatsoever. This was one of those times for Jennifer that being cross was effortless. While she thought Simeon to be wonderfully wise and, well, brilliant, his half-answers and vague explanations were becoming quite an annoyance.

The Shailma’s latest speech had left her perturbed. Furthermore, she noticed that when she began to feel less perturbed, all she needed to do was let a few lines from his recent lecture wander through her mind and she’d be right back to the greatest height of perturbedness all over again.

Now, it needs to be understood that Jennifer very much enjoyed having a twin brother. Her friends would regularly tell her how fortunate she was and that they, too, wished they had a twin, giving her many opportunities to feel a little superior to them. Jennifer and Judah did have a closer-than-normal relationship and most times it was fun to finish each other's sentences or feel the same kinds of feelings at the same time. There were even times when they'd dream the same dream and almost every time that happened it was ridiculously fun.

Be that as it may, in the two years since their parents' accident, it seemed they shared dreams much more frequently, but the fun had somehow faded. Just last Saturday, in fact, the twins were sitting in the kitchen having breakfast with Bella, when Judah began telling the girls about a very perplexing dream he'd had.

"… And the Prince and Princess lived in this enormous castle, but it had no sides, no walls anywhere in the whole castle." He waved his hands wildly around as if that would help the girls understand his explanation more clearly.

It did not.

"I kept looking around trying to figure it out, but all I could see was that the ceilings on each level hovered in mid-air, while the floors above them rested on the ceiling below it." The explanation went on and on, far too long for Jennifer's liking.

She only half-listened and focused more on digging the raisins out of her porridge.

Bella, on the other hand, had set her spoon down and seemed intrigued by Judah's silly dream. Their auntie had a certain way, sometimes, of listening to stories as though what you were saying was the most important thing ever said.

"How very odd," she replied. "Mhm. Go on, Judah."

"It made no sense, auntie, because there were a floor and a ceiling in every room, on every level, and there were many levels. But on the very top level was an ordinary castle top with the pointy red roof and the window for the damsel in distress where she might throw her hair down to let the hero climb up and rescue her."

"Like Rapunzel!" Bella said, acting curiouser and curiouser.

"I suppose," Judah nodded. "Not that anyone would ever need rescuing. Since there were no walls, she couldn't be trapped, I suppose."

Judah continued rambling on and on, throwing in pointless details while leaving out other more important ones. Jennifer was listening but hadn't said a word until the part where Judah began talking about the red sky and how the entire scene—palace, sky, Princess and all—was enclosed in a little glass ball.

"Like a snow globe," he added, trying hard to describe the entire scene. He took a big mouthful of oatmeal and Jennifer saw her chance to finish the dream and annoy her brother.

She saw the opportunity she'd been waiting for and piped up quickly.

"And the Prince and Princess both turned into old raggedy dolls, and the palace became a broken down dollhouse, and the whole thing was not real at all. It was just a game two little girls were playing with their toys. Right, Judah? The game ended, and all the toys went back into the toy box in the corner of their room."

Judah glared across the table. He hated when Jennifer would finish his dreams. It ruined them completely. It was far worse than when someone would tell the punch line to one of his jokes before he could get to it. He banged his fists on the table, causing Bella to jump.

"Jennifer," he shouted. "Stop doing that!"

Even though he tried to sound angry, he was smirking a bit because both Judah and Jennifer knew perfectly well that if one finished the explanation of the other's dream, then they had both dreamed the same dream. Both also knew perfectly well that non-twins never had such an experience and they loved being different than everyone else. It was just one of those "twin things" they loved and hated all at the same time.

There were some things about being twins they loved altogether, and then there were a few other things they hated completely. Countless other things fit somewhere in the middle. But this? Simeon's ridiculous speech? This was much more of a nightmare than a dream of any sort. This would not fit on the love/hate scale anywhere. It was intolerable. Jennifer hated the speech and wished she could erase it from her mind.

Jennifer loved Judah; she did. But he was not the least bit dependable; completely unreliable. She certainly did not want to have to count on him for her safety or to hear things she didn't hear or to see things she might miss. But most of all, she did not want to depend on anyone to get her out of Trilleah. Just because she knew these horrible bits of information about the Twins needing each other did not mean that Judah knew them as well.

"What if I know such things and Judah doesn't?" she squealed in panic.

"Rant if you wish, Little One," Simeon said patiently. "Do you believe that you are the only one who hears their Shailma? Do you believe that I am the only Shailma who gives wisdom and correction to my mortal? Do you not know by now that everyone hears from their Shailmas?" Truthfully, it wasn't something she had spent too much time considering … until now.

"Jennifer," Simeon continued, sharper than she cared for. "This is your third trip into Trilleah. You ought to have learned by now that I give you specific knowledge before entering Trilleah for your good, for your safety. Do you believe the other mortals will not have the same assistance you receive?"

Simeon was certainly on a role of reprimanding Jennifer. She was becoming increasingly perturbed with him, yet a little thankful as well. After all, Simeon was right in what he said; he always was.

She glanced at the others and watched for a few moments. Jennifer never had this opportunity before to see the others with their Shailmas and now, taking her mind off of herself and considering the others, she thought it looked like they were each focusing intently. She assumed it was because they were having their own conversations with their own Shailmas. Jennifer was satisfied that Judah would be given the same information after all. She would simply have to trust him, for truly, she had no other option.

"LOOK!"

Jennifer heard a loud shout and looked over to see Matt pointing ahead. Everyone turned to where his finger was pointing and there it was.

Trilleah.

Solstice had opened its gates again to the Travelers. Her belly churned a little, and both a nervous agitation and a peaceful assurance fought within her for the top spot. There seemed to be something different about the gates this time. She reminded herself it was Winter Solstice and that perhaps it was a bit colder than normal. This idea did not explain the icy feeling that hovered in the air, however, and she kept looking for a better one. It was the same chilly feeling that had been with them back home all winter long. She had no reasonable explanation then, and she certainly could come up with none now.

As Jennifer looked intently at the gates, the dark eyes suddenly made an appearance in her mind and she heard a whisper, but couldn't make out the words.

She was finally close enough to Judah for him to be able to hear her, so she asked if he also felt the cold agitation in the air or if he'd heard any mumbling words or seen any gray eyes behind his own. Jennifer hoped he hadn't, and that it was nothing more than her nervousness. Her hope was quickly dismissed.

"I sure do feel something in the air. It's getting thicker the closer we get to the gate. I don't hear any mumbling, though," Judah said. "Seems like there are too many shadows around it. Look!" he pointed toward the gates, now very close. As Jennifer squinted her eyes to see what her brother was pointing at, the shadows became clearly visible.

"Maybe it's just something we've never noticed before. I haven't paid attention to this side of the gates before, have you?" Jennifer asked. "It's usually dark on this side of the gates."

"Maybe it's nothing. I'm sure it is nothing at all, Jelly Bean, don't worry about it," Judah replied. She knew he was only trying to keep her calm, but it wasn't working; any grains of calm were far from Jennifer by now.

She was about to call to Bella, who also seemed to notice something unusual surrounding the gates, but as she opened her mouth she heard Simeon instead. His voice had once again moved into her mind, which is where she heard him.

Hush now, Little One. It is not the time for hollering or drawing attention to yourself.

"Why not?" she shot back.

Remain quiet. Don't ask any more questions. Simeon sounded a little less patient than usual, so she decided he was quite serious.

Hush yourself now, Little One.

Jennifer hushed herself, at least on the outside, but on the inside, it was certainly not hushed; not anything even close to hushed. On the inside, she was in a full-fledged panic. Not only was something thick and dark surrounding the gates, but there was also something dark and sinister that continued to peer through her eyes. To add to this outrageous combination of fear and panic, Simeon's earlier words caused her to be aware that something yet unforeseen was awaiting them.

Jennifer realized that she had only been to Trilleah two times before now, but in her recollection, this trip through the portal was taking an extraordinarily long time. It felt like they should have been through the gates by now, greeting the other Travelers inside of Asphelia's Hollow. She knew that each trip before this one they would have passed straight through the Solstice Gates and into Malleana Forest without any notice of anything. This was clearly not happening today.

As they were right at the gates now, it was clear there was some slimy film stretched across it—like a spider's web. Something was wound throughout the entirety of the gates and while they could see it was there, it wasn't apparent if the web—or whatever it was—was strong enough to keep them out of Trilleah altogether.

Judah, now very close to Jennifer, called to her. While they were twins and born within minutes of one another, Judah had the nature of an older brother and she now felt very much like the baby sister.

"Jelly Bean, when we get home, I have some great things to show you that I found in the basement this morning," he offered. Jennifer didn't care.

"IF we get home that is," she snapped.

Now Judah was not one to give up easily and, in fact, some might suggest him to be wildly stubborn, much like their daddy had been.

"Oh, don't be ridiculous, it's just a little slime; nothing the Elliot Twins can't handle."

She gave up. Jennifer would never be able to out-stubborn her brother. "Oh, Judah, fine. If you say so." Judah winked and nodded at her; they both tightened their grip.

Quite unexpectedly, although everything was quite unexpected in these odd flashes of time, all the Shailmas and their mortals hung back … except for Matt. He and Mishan picked up speed and went by the slimy gates so quickly that it was hard to see them at all. Then suddenly, Matt was back with the rest of them.

"The slime is from King Shrailzhar. Mishan says it is not designed to keep us out and we can go right through; it won't stop us. However, it *is* designed to cling to us and slow us down enough that the armies can catch up and overtake us. Apparently, the king has figured out how we have been getting into Trilleah and he is determined to stop us.

"Since he cannot harness the sun and keep the Solstice days from coming, he is powerless to stop the gates from opening. I suppose this is his best shot at stopping us."

Of course, this was King Shrailzhar's best shot at keeping them out of his land, although, he had set up unspeakable horrors that he could inflict upon them inside the gates ... if the Travelers got through—horrors that would ensure those dreadful Curse Breakers would never leave his dark land of Trilleah, or the cursed forest, again.

Outflying a Flyer

chapter eleven

The group was hushed. Nobody was sure if the others were quiet because they were without anything to say or because each was desperately tuned to their Shailma. Some were overwhelmed with fear.

Before too much time passed, Judah spoke up. "Here's what we need to do. Jennifer, your Shailma is the fastest, so you are going to go through first. Don't worry, the rest of us will be right behind you. We'll all go through together but will avoid the slime because you, Jelly Bean, will tear it down."

He did not give her any time to respond, knowing if he did that he'd have a full-fledged fight on his hands, and there was no time for such things.

"At the very instant we are through the gates, we will all go different directions, completely passing over Malleana Forest. It seems King Shrailzhar has figured out that's where we arrive, and he has his entire army waiting for us.

"Instead, we will go *over* the forest. Once we are spotted, which won't take the army long, we will spread out and go in different directions. Jennifer, you will go to the north, Bella to the south, Matt you head to the west and I'll go back toward the east. I think the king's riders will get confused and twist themselves into a state, leaving them unable to follow any of us … or … I hope that's what will happen."

"Where are we going to settle then, if not in the forest?" Jennifer asked. She was sure that Judah's Shailma must be directing such plans to him, for certainly he had no idea how to confuse the king's riders, and have them "twist themselves into a state."

Matt piped in. "When none of the king's riders are after us —and we must be absolutely, positively, without a doubt certain that they are not—we will meet in the hollow. The Shailmas will put us directly in front of the entrance rock. Take no time, but step straightaway into the hole and get inside the hollow."

"What if we can't shake Shrailzhar's riders?" Bella asked, her voice sounding flimsy.

"Bella," Matt spoke with phony confidence, "our Shailmas are much wiser than the king's flyers. Don't concern yourself with things that are out of our control. While we may not know what to do, our Shailmas are perfectly capable of such a thing as this. They will know what to do."

Finally, Judah spoke one last statement, leaving Jennifer puzzled as to where his wisdom came from on days such as today.

"Hey now," he shouted, "it's the Shailma's job to get us inside and to the hollow." He looked directly at Jennifer as he finished the thought. "It is our jobs to trust them." With those final words and a few confident winks and head nods from Judah and Matt, they raced toward the Solstice Gates.

"Hang on," Simeon whispered. His words were so powerful and came so quickly, that Jennifer couldn't tell if she heard him with her ears or inside the limits of her mind. Either way, she did hear him loud and clear, and she had no problem in obeying this command.

She dug her fingers deep into Simeon's coat and leaned down as low as she could until her cheek was touching his back. Jennifer dug her feet into his sides and used every muscle in her body to cling tightly to the Shailma.

Not only did she want to hang on with all her might, but she hoped that if she could get close enough to him, she might somehow be able to blend into him and the armies might not notice her.

She had heard stories about the dullness of both the armies and Shrailzhar's flyers. Just the evening before at her birthday party—after all the guests had gone—Matt and Bella were questioning whether those in Shrailzhar's Armies had a soul … or a brain. The answer seemed to be that they could not have a soul, for it would have long been captured by the king himself, and they most certainly could not have a brain, for their dullness was great.

Simeon pulled his enormous wings in, folding them into himself. He used his smaller ones to fly; something Jennifer had not seen before now. In the twinkle of an eye, Jennifer and Simeon tore through the gates; the slime that blanketed them was thick and cumbersome. It slowed them instantly, and Jennifer felt a jolt of panic bolt through her.

Unlike the slime, which covered much of Simeon but missed most of Jennifer, the panic did not miss her. It had enveloped her and felt closer than the stale air that was filling her lungs. It felt like the same coldness that had covered her when she awoke yesterday—maybe it was.

"Go, Simeon … GO," she kept repeating under her breath. Once through the gates, Simeon again stretched wide his gigantic wings. The smaller ones were so slime covered that they were useless. With these enormous wings, Simeon glided effortlessly through the air, slime and all, and in no time, the king's flyers who had been right behind them, fell away. Simeon was able to move quickly toward the hollow now. Much of the panic fell away, leaving Jennifer to feel a great rush of calm drape over her. She heard something familiar behind her and peeked under her arm, finding a delightful sight.

Sam! Sam had joined them. She wondered when he had arrived and if he was somehow aware of the plans to confuse the king's flyers. This was not the time to ask or even waste any time caring about. Even if Jennifer did yell out to Sam, he'd never have heard her over the deafening ruckus of entering Trilleah. She would ask him later, in the hollow.

It was noticeable that Sam and his Shailma had very few of the flyers behind them, but more than were behind Jennifer and Simeon. She strained her eyes to see where they had all gone and saw that Judah had attracted a large number—most of them, in fact. Judah's Shailma zipped this way and darted that way, but the flyers stayed right with them. Not even one fell away.

There was still a vast number of the armies back in the forest as well, waiting for the flyers to bring back any Curse Breakers they might capture. However, that looked now like it wasn't going to happen at all; the flyers were nowhere to be seen. Of course, neither were any of the others who had entered the gates with Jennifer. She was suddenly alone with Simeon.

Do not worry yourself; we are going to the hollow now. Get ready, Jenny. She had to think back to the plan and try to retrieve the part of what she was to do when Simeon reached the rock leading to the hollow.

Ah, yes, she remembered. All she needed to do was dash into the hollow. Even before she had fully retrieved the information, she heard Simeon shout.

"Go, Jenny. NOW!" and go she did. This was not a time she needed to be told twice, nor did she ask questions demanding to know the reason behind the command. Immediately she put her foot into the small hole under the rock and was pulled into the hollow.

When she opened her eyes, the face she saw was not one she had expected. It was not Judah or Bella or Matt; not even Sam. The face looking back at her belonged to Miriam.

Their eyes met instantly, and they both realized that they had startled the other. The two stared at each other and for a moment, neither was sure what to say. Miriam was the first to break the awkward silence.

"You … uh … you are not who I expected," she said.

"Who did you expect?" Jennifer asked.

"Well," Miriam thought for a moment. "I'm not sure, but it wasn't you." Jennifer must have had an odd look on her face because Miriam immediately added, "not that I'd hoped for anyone in particular, and I am just as satisfied to see you as anyone else … I suppose."

Now Jennifer was curiously confused. Was Miriam annoyed or glad that she was the first to arrive at the hollow? Nonetheless, it didn't matter. What did matter to Jennifer, was HOW Miriam got here before her … before any of them.

"Miriam, uh, when did you arrive?" she asked nonchalantly, trying to seem indifferent to the answer but desperately wanting to know. An ugly suspicion churned in Jennifer's stomach.

"About one second before you did, I suppose," Miriam replied.

"Well, I'm curious as to how you got through the gates. Didn't you have to go through the slime? If you arrived before I did, I'd expect that you had to come through the slime." Even as Jennifer was speaking, it came to her that something was off. Something was not right about this situation. The churning in her stomach turned sour.

"Jennifer, you went through the slime so no, of course, I didn't have to." Miriam looked at her in a way that made Jennifer even more confused. Her tone was full of disgust and dislike for everything that had to do with Jennifer.

"So you came in after me?" she asked.

"Of course, I came in after you. I came through the gates the same time as everyone else. I didn't know there was any specific plan or order. My Shailma noticed the armies in the forest, so didn't drop me there. Instead, we came straight to the hollow." Miriam moved closer to the eating stump where the basket of tiles was sitting and set a couple of the clay tablets that had been in her hand this whole time, back into the basket. "I arrived here only seconds before you did, just like I said."

Jennifer wanted to ask why she had some of the clay tablets and how, if she'd arrived only seconds before, she had time to grab any of the tablets and move so far from the eating stump. It seemed like Miriam had been here a while longer than a couple of seconds. There was no time to argue with her now, though, because right then both Sam and Matt came crashing into the hollow.

"Oh, I'm glad to see you two," Jennifer squealed. "Have you seen Judah?"

"I saw him a second ago," Sam piped up. "He looked as though he was having a bit of fun, and I'd expect him here any minute now."

"I hope so," Jennifer whined. "I'm getting worried." Then, just in case the boys had missed the obvious, she added, "Oh, look who was already here when I got to the hollow." Jennifer nodded toward Miriam, who was ignoring them and instead, digging curiously through the tiles. Countless things began to run through Jennifer's suspicious mind about Miriam. How did she get to the hollow first? Why did she seem to know Pierce from somewhere other than Trilleah? Why did she have clay tiles in her hand when Jennifer had come in and why was she digging through them again now?

As she gave attention to all the thoughts that danced in her head, the gray eyes reappeared and seemed to be more interested in Miriam than Jennifer was herself. For a moment, it looked as though Miriam saw those gray eyes; she stopped what she was doing and stared, just for a second. At that moment, an excruciatingly sharp pain pierced Jennifer's eyes. She drew her breath in sharply and let out a horrendous squeal.

Not Fast Enough

chapter twelve

A long while passed without anyone else tumbling into the hollow.

"Where are the others?" Sam finally asked out loud what the rest were thinking silently.

"Don't worry, Sam," Jennifer said, digging her fingers playfully into his hair and scratching his head. "They'll be along any minute now. I know they will." The truth was that Jennifer was becoming extremely worried herself, but sometimes when you try to calm someone else's worry, your own worry calms a little as well.

Sam poked her in the ribs. "I know; I was just wondering." The concern had left his voice and he began to sing at the top of his lungs, which would have been wonderful if he could carry a tune which, he most certainly could not. Jennifer picked a few pieces of leaves out of his crazy hair and added her voice to his. The duet rang loudly through the hollow, filling up chambers and bouncing off walls.

"Ooooooh … Hey diddle diddle, the cat and the fiddle, and a cow jumping over the moon, the little dog laughed to see such a sight and the dish ran away with the spoooooon."

Jennifer noticed a mop and broom in the corner and ran over, grabbing one in each hand. She tossed the mop to Sam, and kept the broom, and together their voices rang out even louder. The longer they waited for the other Travelers, the more silly their songs became. On and on they went, singing and dancing around the room and for a few minutes they traded the apprehension of Trilleah for childhood silliness and off-key singing. Sam, after all, was the most fun-loving, crazy kind of boy Jennifer had ever known.

Matt had sat down at the eating stump and was delighted by their antics. He leaned back in his chair and booed and cheered all the while laughing until his stomach ached. Miriam, on the other hand, became perturbed with their shenanigans and had left the Chamber. Perhaps it was because she was immune to fun, maybe she had something more important to do, or possibly because she was Miriam, who didn't play well with others. Whatever the reason for her departure, the others were satisfied with the group of three that remained.

Somewhere in between the third and fourth verses of yet another silly song, the duet was interrupted.

"Thankfully so," according to Matt. The loud commotion filing into the hollow was a welcome distraction as Bella, and then Pierce, tumbled inside.

It took a knack and a whole lot of good timing to get into the hollow without tumbling, as Jennifer had learned on her first visit. She figured so far that she'd just been lucky.

She thought back to her first time here and how the three boys tumbled through the entry, landing in one big heap, and how she laughed until her belly hurt. She wished that Pierce would have repeated that entrance now because she enjoyed laughing at his follies. She probably should not have enjoyed his missteps as much as she did, however, since most often when she was in danger it was Pierce who rescued her. Jennifer hadn't realized it until now.

Oh well, she told herself and decided that she would continue to laugh at the grouchy boy as often as such opportunities presented themselves.

"Did either of you see Judah? He's not here yet," Jennifer puffed, still catching her breath from the rambunctious duet. Suddenly, great worry came plowing back into her mind.

Pierce said nothing, of course, but Bella *hmm'd* for a minute before she replied. "I did see him earlier but not recently. He'll be here any minute, I'm sure. Don't worry," she said, tweaking the end of Jennifer's nose and then Sam's. "I see I missed a concert?" she asked, pointing toward the makeshift microphones.

"Oh, Bella, you did," Matt said, banging his fist down on the table. "It was the concert of a lifetime, and I had a front-row seat," he announced, putting on his most serious of faces. "But, only those with the quickest Shailmas were able to hear it, I'm afraid. You obviously have one of the slower ones; poor dear."

One thing about Matt; he was a very kind, handsome, and altogether lovely boy, but if there was one thing he didn't have, it was the ability to be funny—ever. Oh, he tried, but most often whoever was around at the moment just looked at him rather puzzled, not completely sure if he intended to be funny at all. This moment was no different.

"You do know, Matt, that the speed of the Shailmas had nothing to do with our arriving at the hollow before the rest, don't you?" Miriam asked. Apparently, she had re-joined them without being noticed and took them all by surprise; one of the many things that annoyed the others about her.

"Well yes, Miriam, I do," Matt said. "I was teasing."

"Oh," Miriam answered. "I couldn't tell," she said flatly.

Any bit of fun they were having was over. Miriam made sure of that for she had a natural gift, so it seemed, to suck the fun out of any situation where it looked like someone may be having some … fun that is … Miriam was clearly against it.

Now they were not entirely sure what to do. The Travelers didn't know when Judah might arrive nor who else, if anyone, may join them. Bella looked at her watch, and her niece took notice.

"I wonder where Judah is?" Jennifer huffed, pacing back and forth. "I wish there were windows in this stupid hollow."

It was not simply by chance there were no windows in the hollow, but rather by some divine planning, for if one could see out, that would mean that one could also see in. It might seem, at first, that the reason there were no windows in the hollow was so that predators could not see in, since it was a place of secrecy and safety. However, the truth of the matter was the exact opposite. The walls were solid rock and mud, without windows or cracks or peepholes whatsoever, to keep the Travelers from seeing out.

If the Travelers could see out on this particular Winter Solstice morning, they would be fainthearted by what they would have seen. Jennifer especially, the one who had wished for a window, would have been altogether unsatisfied with what a window would have revealed.

Judah, who had been particularly close to his Shailma and was known by the other Travelers for having an unusually significant amount of trust in him, was having a hard time trusting him now. It appeared that the Armies of Shrailzhar had considered that the Travelers might suspect something was up and, therefore, had come up with a suspicious plan of their own.

The one reason the Shailmas and their Travelers had managed to outrun the army of flyers so easily and reach the hollow unsuspected was not because of their great speed. The fact was, rather, that the armies had decided they would gather together and follow one Traveler, endeavoring to trap that one. Judah was who they decided to chase after and now, if Jennifer could have seen out of a window, she would have found the entire army of Shrailzhar's flyers chasing hard after her brother—about to overtake him.

Shemaiah had been in worse situations before this, however, and as Judah talked back and forth with his Shailma, he remained surprisingly calm. Although, he didn't know that all the other Travelers had already reached the hollow and assumed, as anyone in his situation might, that they were all out and about, somewhere, also being chased by Shrailzhar's flyers.

When Judah was younger, much younger than now, he seemed to have an ability to find all sorts of unusual and dangerous situations to get himself into. As quiet and timid as Jennifer was, Judah was the opposite. "It seems that Judah has the curiosity of both the twins," their mamma would often say. Daddy would always agree, adding his thoughts about Judah's spirited ways.

"He's all boy, Molly," Theo would laugh. "It's a wonder he makes it to bedtime each day." They would laugh and discuss how twins could be so very different. Theo would often add something ridiculous, like maybe they mixed the twins up and took someone else's boy home and, in fact, poor Jennifer's twin was living with another family somewhere else.

This use to annoy Judah because all of the teasing made him wonder if maybe they preferred Jennifer's quietness over his rambunctiousness; her timidity over his bravery.

Now, today in this particular precarious predicament Judah found himself in, it appeared that his father would finally have been right, and he may not make it through this day. It also seemed that his brave heart only went so far, and now he was, indeed, becoming quite afraid.

What Lies Behind

*J*udah, Shemaiah uttered silently, *you are full of bravery, and I am carrying you. Do not be afraid; you ARE valiant and you ARE a mighty warrior.*

I don't feel valiant, Judah thought.

Oh, but feelings are not always truth now, are they? asked Shemaiah. Back and forth their thoughts mingled, weaving around each other and doing an empowering sort of dance in Judah's mind.

The more Shemaiah reminded Judah of his warrior spirit, the more courageous Judah became.

I cannot take you to the hollow until the king's flyers have gone, yet I cannot shake them like this. Then, a rather odd question entered into his mind. *Judah, do you trust me?*

Of course, came the boy's silent response. *You know I've trusted you since that day when I was only two years old when you kept me from drowning.* Judah knew that his Shailma was aware of his great trust in him and was somewhat confused, and even slightly saddened that Shemaiah would need to ask such a question at all.

Judah's memories wandered back to the first time he'd seen his Shailma. He recalled every detail. Way back when the twins were only two years old, their parents had taken them camping at a remote spot in the wilderness. The spot wasn't particularly meant for camping, however, their daddy was never much for things to be as they were supposed to be. Not in the least. Their daddy didn't enjoy living within boundaries of society or by rules of others and he often ended up in hot water for living by his own rules. He was always looking for an adventure for his family, and this particular trip he'd found more of an adventure than he had hoped for.

Theo had found the perfect spot for camping and was busily setting up their tent and working on building a campfire while Molly entertained the twins. Not feeling well at the time, she wasn't too quick on her feet. She preferred sitting to running that particular day.

Jennifer had decided she was going to be grumpy on this day of camping and was demanding snacks from the car. While Molly was digging around the back seat beneath bags and suitcases, Judah ran to his daddy. Unfortunately, rather than going toward him, Judah ran in the opposite direction of where he thought Daddy was.

He ran and ran and ran. Now, Judah may have realized he wasn't finding his daddy and eventually may have turned around or sat down and cried. However, something else caught his attention and the noisy, bubbling river mesmerized the young boy. He forgot all about where he was heading or why he was heading there.

When Mamma realized Judah was gone, she became hysterical, screaming and hollering. Daddy swooped Jennifer up in his arms and the three of them went searching for Judah. Quite suddenly, Molly stopped and grabbed Theo's arm. She was panicked but did not want to shout again lest she frightened her little boy, startling him.

Daddy looked to where Mamma was pointing. Sure enough —there was Judah, standing on a rock at the edge of a ferocious river. He had picked up a handful of rocks and was happily throwing them, one by one, into the water. As each one hit the river and made a splash, Judah would jump up and down with excitement. The slightest misstep and Judah would topple into the water, be washed downstream and gone forever.

"Oh, dear God," Molly whispered.

What neither Mamma nor Daddy knew, was that Judah had seen his Shailma. That was the first time Shemaiah had made himself known to Judah, and the Shailma kept Judah safe until Theo could come and sweep the boy up under his arm.

Now, it's well known by anyone who knows anything at all about Shailmas, that the magnificent beings are not usually visible and definitely not supposed to be seen. However, every once in awhile, and then only when absolutely necessary, a Shailma may open the eyes of the one for whom they are responsible. This had been, undoubtedly, one of those times.

Shemaiah and Judah had become close since that day, with Judah needing to be rescued countless times since the river incident.

Today seemed like one of those times, here in Trilleah, but for the first time since Judah was two years old, he doubted Shemaiah's ability to keep him safe, and he was deathly afraid.

Judah, do you trust me? The Shailma asked his fearful mortal again, startling the boy back from his memories.

I trust you. Even though I'm afraid, I trust you to get me to the hollow, Judah replied. At the bottom of his stomach, fear made him churn and he wanted to throw up. But at the bottom of his soul, he knew Shemaiah would do whatever was required to keep him safe.

"OK … hold on!" Shemaiah whispered. Judah tightened his grip and laid a little lower against Shemaiah. He hung on fiercely. All at once, Shemaiah turned and instead of being followed by the army of Shrailzhar's flyers, the Shailma and his rider were facing them; ALL of them.

If Judah had not closed his eyes tightly, too afraid to see the great number that was coming against them, he would have seen the looks of dread that spread across their faces as Shemaiah turned to face them. In less than three seconds, the entire army of flyers turned in mid-air. Instead of being the pursuers, they had become the ones being pursued.

Judah became curious as their speed picked up and he could feel, even with his eyes closed, that they were going tremendously fast. He opened one eye just a crack and peered out. Immediately he saw that the wicked army of flyers was in front of them, and they were speeding madly away.

How did this happen? he wondered. *Why would a massive army like the one he was now seeing, suddenly turn and retreat from one lone Shailma?* This was not making sense to Judah and he wished he'd had kept his eyes open. What he saw now puzzled him, for he was only looking ahead. If he had been able to see behind, he would have seen another army—one far greater than the one in front of him—had joined him and Shemaiah.

At least two thousand in number, the Shamar Shailmas had come to their rescue and easily overpowered the meek army of flyers. Shrailzhar's army of flyers quickly returned to their place on the ground just beyond the forest, and Shemaiah could now take Judah to the foot of the hollow and deliver him safely.

"Thank you for trusting," the tired Shailma said as Judah slipped his foot into the entrance. Judah turned back to look at what was still blazed into his memory, but every Shailma, both seen and unseen, the Shamars, and his own great Shemaiah, were gone. At least, they were out of sight.

Judah turned back and entered Asphelia's Hollow without excitement or feelings of any sort, for there was something else weighing far too heavy on his mind.

One Bright Light

chapter fourteen

Shemaiah had asked Judah if he trusted him just before the Shailma had turned and changed the direction of the entire situation and saved Judah. Why did he ask? Did the Shailma's course of action depend on Judah's answer? What if Judah's answer had been different? What if Judah had said that he did not trust Shemaiah? Did trusting in Shemaiah somehow give the Shailma an authority to act?

The tumbling thoughts, none of which he figured would have reasonable answers, piled up, one on top of the next, in Judah's mind. The boy was so distracted by the growing collection of wonderings that he did not even notice the loud, exuberant cheers which rang out as he stumbled into the hollow. And stumble he did.

The Travelers, it appeared, had gathered around the eating stump and some were playing a game. It was a useless attempt to distract themselves from swirling fears and nagging ponderings about Judah. So naturally, when he finally tumbled into the hollow, the game was forgotten and squeals of excitement filled the air.

Judah's sister was by far the most excited and ran to help him up from the ground. "We should put a rubber mat at the bottom of this stupid entrance," Judah said, and everyone agreed.

All the while Jennifer was brushing dirt from Judah's T-shirt and rambling on about how she was so worried, and cursing the hollow for having no windows, Judah was wondering if he should tell Jennifer—or any of the Travelers for that matter—about what had happened. How Shemaiah had asked about trusting him or how they had turned and headed straight into the face of the king's flyers, chasing them back to their place in the forest.

He decided against it for now and instead turned his attention to his rambling sister. Judah pretended to listen intently to Jennifer and nodded, mumbling things like "mhm," and "Oh, really." He so easily fooled her that sometimes it made him chuckle and other times her naivety weighed heavily on him.

Judah ran his fingers through his hair, trying to straighten it out without much success. He wondered if he looked like he always looked, or if his experience had changed his reflection somehow. After nodding a quick hello to everyone, he excused himself and disappeared through one of the passageways offering a polite, "I'll be right back," to the curious on-lookers.

"He seems curiously serious," Sam mentioned to whoever wanted to listen.

"He's usually pretty serious," Jennifer replied. She had been so busy telling Judah about what she'd been thinking, feeling, and considering while waiting for him, that she never took even the smallest second to pay attention to Judah or what he might have to say. Come to think of it, she never gave him a chance to say anything whatsoever.

"I've never noticed him be too serious, Jenny," Sam said. "He's usually cheeky and hilariously witty. He makes me laugh."

"That's how I've noticed him as well," added Miriam. She thought a moment and then added, "but not this time." One by one, each Traveler nodded in agreement and Jennifer wondered how she could have missed something that everyone else found so obvious. She never found him to be all that hilarious or witty.

"Why didn't anyone ask him about it then?" she said, annoyed. Truthfully, as she listened to everyone go on about it, she felt more and more poorly about her selfish behavior. She vowed to talk less and listen more. As the girl was making a mental list of things she was determined to do differently, everyone got up from the eating stump and began murmuring. Jennifer looked around to see what had grabbed their attention and saw that Judah had returned.

"Judah," Bella's voice rose above the rest. "Are you OK? You seem a bit … a bit … well, a bit off." She always sounded so sincere rather than nosey or curious. Perhaps it was all the same thing in the end.

"Ya, you seem freaked out," Sam blurted. He moved to stand so close to Judah that it struck the others as comical.

"Sam, let him breathe," Miriam snarled.

"What happened?" Sam asked before moving away only a few inches. He threw a glare in Miriam's direction as he shuffled his feet.

"I'm fine," Judah said although, in truth, he was not fine. He kept playing the situation over and over. Each time he watched the story replay itself on the screen in his mind, more questions arose. Since there seemed to be no answers for any of them, he just added each to the pile that was growing in his mind. The one that was being added at this moment was whether or not he should reveal to his fellow Travelers what he'd experienced or just how much, if anything at all, he should share. He felt as though he had to give *some* explanation for his distractedness.

"I had a tough time getting here," he said. "The flyers were bigger and faster than I expected. It took some maneuvering by my Shailma to lose them and get me to the hollow."

There. Hopefully, that brief reasoning would turn their attention away from him and onto something else, at least while he was deciding if he should reveal more of his experience and to whom he should reveal it.

"So, what's the plan?" Sam asked loudly, shifting the attention from Judah to their reason for being here in the first place. He seemed to grow more impatient with each new journey. "*Is* there a plan?" he huffed.

"There's always a plan," Jennifer responded, surprised that it came from her mouth, since she wasn't thinking about responding in her head; it just fell from her lips. "We don't always know what it is or which way we should go or how we will get to where we need to be, but Sam, there is always a plan." Jennifer stepped back, surprising herself more than anyone, although it appeared from the looks on the faces looking back at her own, she'd surprised more than just herself.

Now, Jennifer was not keen on attention and it seemed like right now she was receiving far too much of it.

I need to get away from these staring eyes, she thought, and slowly edged her way to one of the doorways in the hollow. It was an entranceway Jennifer hadn't gone through before and now that she noticed where she was standing, she realized she'd not seen anyone else go through it either. Jennifer supposed that could be a good thing or perhaps, not so good of a thing. Nevertheless, she was here now and it was the closest escape. Since the eyes were still gazing at her, Jennifer made one final comment to divert their stares before darting through the opening in the side of the rock.

"I wonder, Judah, if your long delay was part of the plan or if it was, in fact, a distraction from the plan." A few eyes turned toward Judah, but not all of them, so she added one more sentence that she was certain would turn the rest. "What do you think about that, Judah?" Again, the thought was not anything she had been thinking about, and so again, she wondered from where it had come.

Nevertheless, with all eyes now shifted toward her brother, she took the opportunity to dart through the carved out entrance and into the passageway. It was small; so small she felt like she wanted to step right back out of it, but before she could do so, something caught her eye and made her curious. A light; or at least what she thought was a light.

The light was not being thrown from any of the lanterns, and it was white. And small. It was no bigger than the point of a pencil, but it was blindingly bright, so bright that it caught her attention immediately, and she couldn't look away.

Jennifer took a step toward it, then another, and one after that. Before she knew it she had moved halfway down the passageway. It was as though the light was calling to her, beckoning her to come. She couldn't tell if the light was moving away from her or if it was just so far down the passageway that she had a great distance to go before reaching it.

Her feet carried her a long way it seemed, but the light never got any bigger … or any closer. It made no sense. Nevertheless, Jennifer continued to move toward it, growing curiouser and curiouser and thinking she might be somehow hearing the light calling to her. Light does not have a voice; she knew that. She also knew that something about this light was beckoning her.

It was chilly in the small space and as she shivered a little, she tried to recall another time in the hollow when she'd been so cold. She could think of none, but the icy chill did, absolutely, without any doubt whatsoever, remind her of what had been hanging in the air of their little yellow house back in Westlock all this time.

She shivered again; not from the chill this time but from the sudden awareness that she was not alone here and she most certainly had not been alone back home.

Into the Dark

chapter fifteen

Jennifer was startled by a familiar voice behind her.

"Jelly Bean," the voice whispered, as though afraid to speak too loudly in case someone else might hear his words. She knew it was Judah; he was the only one ever to call her by such a silly name.

Without turning around or taking her eyes off of the light, she moved her head so her voice would carry in the right direction. "Judah, I'm right here." She didn't know how close he was, so she whispered as loudly as she could. "Judah, look." She pointed her finger toward the light even though, of course, her brother would never see her gesture in such dimness.

"I see it," he said, now right behind her. She was very glad he'd whispered to her because otherwise, the hand on her back would have shocked her greatly.

"Judah, what is that?" she asked. "I've been walking a long time trying to find the source of that light, but I'm no closer to it now than when I first saw it. It's like there is no end to this passageway."

"I don't know what it is or what's causing it, and I am not feeling too comfortable in here. It's tight … and cold," Judah replied. He tapped her shoulders and asked her, "aren't you cold?" She had been chilly, yes, but the ice that filled her bones in that second was something she'd never be able to explain, for as Judah set his hands on Jennifer's shoulders, she was aware that the hand on her back remained.

"Judah," she whispered without taking any more breaths, now altogether aware of another presence in the passageway, "we need to get out of here … right … NOW!" There was such a panic in her voice that Judah knew she was serious, and he did not take time to ask her why. This was just one of those moments where something inside of him took over and he knew he needed to step up and protect his sister.

"Give me your hand," he said. Jennifer thrust her hand out into the dimness. Judah found it and grabbed tightly to his sister. He couldn't ignore the trembling he felt in her and determined to get her out of there … fast!

Turning around in that small space was tricky and took a bit of maneuvering, mostly because as he turned, Judah squeezed and squished to get his sister in front of him. He didn't know why, because it would have made perfect sense to grasp her hand and lead the way out, but something told him he needed to be between her and the light. That light was not what it had appeared to be. He didn't know anything more than that, but that was all he needed to know.

In this particular passageway, there was no running. It took patience and careful stepping not to trip over one's own feet. Jennifer had no patience left and her breathing was becoming heavy as she tried to move faster than the tight space would allow. Panic was rising within her even though she could no longer feel the hand —or whatever it was that had rested on her back just seconds earlier.

"I can't breathe, Judah," she managed to squeak out.

Judah squeezed her hand and whispered in her ear, "Jelly Bean, calm your insides down. Focus more on breathing and less on moving your feet. Your feet will move on their own." He was still unaware of what had spooked his sister, but it was unquestionable now that something had.

Breathe slowly, a voice in her head whispered. She did. She forced her mind to count slowly as she inhaled and exhaled, inhaled and exhaled, forcing her breathing to slow. *One ... two ... one ... two ...* And on and on it went.

She could see light coming from the Eating Chamber now and it lit up the rest of the passageway bringing a much-needed peace to her belly. A few more steps and she and Judah popped back into the well-lit space. It was only then that Judah could see how white his sister's face had become … as if whatever spooked her had also drained the color from her face and hands, which he now realized were dead cold. Both her hands and her face were as white as snow and frigid as a cold winter morning.

He gently tugged on her hands, stopping her before they were too far inside the Eating Chamber. Judah turned Jennifer around to look directly into her eyes and for a brief moment, Jennifer felt safe. The only other time she had seen such an intense look in her brother's eyes was after they heard the news of their parents' accident.

She was suddenly transported back to that instant when Judah looked her directly in the eyes and said no words with his lips. His eyes, however, told a story; a story that read, *I will keep you safe and protect you. Don't worry; I'm right here.* Now she felt those same words pooling in his eyes and her breathing returned to normal.

"Judah, there was someone else in that passageway. I felt it touch me. I thought it was you, but then you put your hands on my shoulders, and I knew it couldn't be you."

A shiver ran through her skin, sending a tremble from her toes right up her spine and out through the top of her head. As soon as the words were out she wondered if she should have told him or if he'd make fun of her and think she had gone mad. Instead, he continued to hold both her hands in his and stare into her eyes.

"I know. When we were leaving, I saw a pair of red eyes glaring at me. I was sure they were eyes but hoped it was something else; they were angry. When I hear you say this, I know for sure they were eyes." What he didn't tell her was that he'd not put his hands on her shoulders. In fact, he hadn't touched his sister at all until he grabbed her hand to lead her out of the passageway.

Her mind fed no words to her tongue and she just stood there blankly staring at her brother. Jennifer couldn't decide if she should be angry with him for not telling her of the peering eyes, or grateful that he'd kept it to himself until now.

The twins were so entrenched in their feelings and fears and thoughts and words that they hadn't noticed everyone else in the Eating Chamber had stopped their conversations and were watching the twins intently. It was evident to the others that something significant had occurred in their little wanderings down the strange passageway.

"Jelly Bean, we are safe now … it's fine. Let's just stay out of that passageway."

He turned toward the eating stump and immediately noticed the questioning stares of the others. Judah wondered what a sight their faces must have shown and again he was faced—for the second time today—with an unsureness of how much to reveal and how much to keep to himself.

This journey had quickly gone from very bad to a whole lot worse.

Almost Truth

chapter sixteen

"What's going on?" Bella asked. A sort of demanding tone had replaced her usually gentle inquisitiveness. The twins were so deep into the hushed conversation that they were both startled.

Jennifer turned to reply to her auntie, but before she could say anything, Judah, still holding onto her hands, turned her back toward himself and looked her square in the eyes.

"Let me talk, Jennifer," and he nodded a half-nod to her. "Trust me," he added with a look he knew she'd understand.

She began to protest, but Judah squeezed her hand and then let it go. He stepped around Jennifer and walked toward the group. "Did you know that passageway is ridiculously small?" he asked, offering a forced chuckle. "And chilly," he added, pointing toward Sam as he said so.

More than one person tried to respond, and they ended up talking over each other. Being aware that many were talking at the same time, all of them stopped suddenly and looked at one other. Pierce piped up again before anyone else had the chance. "Where did it lead? I've never been down that passageway, although I've wondered about it. Every time I head toward it, something else gets my attention, and I never make it."

"That's what I was going to ask," Sam threw in. He began a bit of a meaningless conversation with Pierce, finding it unusual that they had both tried to wander into the passageway but neither ever made it. While Pierce was annoyed because he wanted to hear Judah's answer, Judah was satisfied with the confusion; it gave him more time to think of how to respond.

"Sam," Bella interrupted. "Shhhh. Let Judah answer the question so we can all stop wondering." All eyes, including Jennifer's, settled on Judah and waited for the answer.

"I'm not sure," was his disappointing reply. "We didn't get too far inside before we decided to come back." Jennifer knew that was not the truth. She had wandered quite far into the mouth of the passageway and it seemed to lead … well, it seemed to lead nowhere at all. Judah looked like he wasn't finished his answer, however, so she waited to see what else he might add.

"The lanterns are different than the other passageways and it was cold." The ears of the Travelers still seemed unsatisfied, so he offered a bit more. "I've never felt cold, or even chilled inside the hollow, but in that passageway, it was very chilly," and as he spoke he nodded toward the entranceway he and Jennifer had just come from. "In fact, that was what Jennifer and I were talking about when we came back here and why I was holding her hands." Judah rubbed his hands together as if trying to warm them … even though they weren't actually cold.

He looked at his sister now, who had a puzzled look on her face, but she said nothing. When Jennifer saw his eyes looking into hers, she knew he had a reason for saying what he did and determined that the very first time she had a chance, she'd ask him about it. Now it was Judah's turn to ask questions—perhaps because he wanted to know some things, or maybe he wanted to steer the conversation in a different direction. Judah had always been good at controlling conversations. He seemed to be able to make them go whichever way he wanted, whenever he wanted to.

Jennifer had often wished she had such a skill, but instead, she was a blurter. She blurted things out before thinking them through and often ended up in conversations she did not wish to be in, wondering how to take back whatever absurd things she'd just spit from her mouth. Now that she was thinking of such things, it made sense why Judah had told her to let him do the talking.

"Why have none of you been down that particular passageway?" he asked the others. Nobody had an answer. They all looked at one other and stammered around, shrugging their shoulders and screwing up their faces.

"That's a good question," Matt said. "I guess we've never had any reason to. At least, I haven't."

That made sense. There were, after all, many entranceways leading away from the Eating Chamber and the Travelers were never in the hollow for long periods of time. When they were inside, they didn't have much free time to wander or investigate, since they were always busy preparing for their journeys.

Now they were all looking around discussing which entranceways each of them had been in, and it turned out that many had been unexplored. It didn't matter much, except Judah had successfully shifted the conversation away from himself. It did, however, make them all curious as to what they may be missing out on and determined that any free time they did have, they would explore the unexplored places.

"That time, I'm afraid," Miriam piped in, "is not now and we *must* get ready for tomorrow's travels."

It seemed that every time Miriam opened her mouth, whether she had something of value to say or not, everyone looked at her as though she was an intrusion or had green skin or scales or two heads. There was something about her that nobody could put a name to; something which caused Miriam to not belong here.

They would all end up wondering the same thing, time after time. *What is she doing here? What is the oddness that is about her?* Nobody ever asked, however, and rarely did they discuss it amongst each other. If they had, they'd have soon learned each of them had the same nervous rolling in their bellies about this odd and unexplained girl. Jennifer knew, though. She knew Miriam wasn't one of them; that she was of Trilleah and not a mortal at all. She knew it but was unable to speak of it or warn the others.

"Well," Bella sighed. "I agree with Miriam. We need to get prepared for tomorrow; I fear it will come early and be a long day."

"The days here in Trilleah seem longer than the ones back home," Sam spoke up. He was beginning to show signs of significant distress it seemed, at coming to Trilleah. "Are you certain, Bella, that the days here are the same length? One day here seems like three or four days back home."

"I agree with you, Sam. However, I can assure you the days here have the same twenty-four hours as the ones back home," Bella answered. "Although," she said, adding another level of confusion, "I'm not sure that the Shailmas don't somehow slow those hours down in order for us to do what needs to be done and get out again before the gates close." They all pondered this idea. The truth was that Bella had no idea how to measure time in

Trilleah, for it was far different than time in Westlock. It was too much to think about, so she never did.

"So, as I was saying," Miriam repeated, "let's get prepared."

"Great idea." Bella looked around the group, deciding which tasks to assign to which Travelers. "I'll make the lunches and drinks for tomorrow but, J, could you and Judah make us some lunch for now?"

Jennifer, still shaken from the hand on her back in that cold, endless passageway, didn't want to do anything except return home. However, she was thankful that Bella had, at least, assigned her task to include Judah. Right now he was the only one Jennifer wanted to be with and the only one who gave her any feeling of safety.

"Yes," she replied.

Judah took her hand as he walked passed and led her to the passageway that would lead them to the kitchen. "It's OK, Jelly Bean," he whispered, hoping no one else would hear his words or notice her odd behavior. "I'm with you, and besides, we have been down this passageway many times. We know it's safe."

"But, Judah," her protests of fear were louder than his whispers of reasoning, "how do you know that thing didn't follow us into the Eating Chamber? How do you know it's not following us now?" She spun her head to look behind her, even though she knew she'd not have seen anything, since the lanterns never shone where they had been—only where they were going. In some unexplainable and nonsensical way, the lanterns only cast light in front of them and even that was only a very few steps at a time. This realization made Jennifer anxious, and she squeezed Judah's hand.

"J," her brother replied, "I am confident that nothing followed us anywhere. In fact," he whispered, "the more I think about it, the more I'm convinced that whatever was in that cold passageway is there to scare any Travelers off. I don't know what that light is that you saw, but I'm absolutely, positively, sure that something does not want us to get to it. I don't know why, or where this feeling is coming from, but I have a hunch the light at the end of that tunnel is something crucial and quite necessary to breaking the curses of the forest. If it is," now it was Judah's turn to squeeze his sister's hand tightly, "then, of course, the land will do whatever it can to keep us from getting to it."

They had arrived at the kitchen by now, and the conversation postponed itself for another time. Jennifer reminded herself not to let the light she'd seen escape from her memory and tucked it away to ponder as time would allow.

Bodiless Beings Unseen

chapter seventeen

Judah opened the fridge and bent down to see what was available to make a lunch with for the bunch of them. Nothing popped out. "What shall we make, sister?" he asked, his head still inside the refrigerator. It seemed increasingly odd how even though there were six months between trips to Trilleah, the fridge was always well-stocked. Nothing ever seemed to go bad, and while Jennifer had considered this many times, no reasonable answers ever came to her.

It was just one of the odd "Trilleah things" that she had decided not to worry about or think on for too long.

Her mood seemed to be improving now that she had something else to focus on, and Judah was glad. He was running out of ways to comfort his sister; his own courage was thinning as well.

The two of them went on for quite some time laughing and making stupid jokes and spouting off meaningless silliness. Jennifer was thankful that her brother was watching out for her. If he weren't afraid, then she wouldn't be either. The truth was, of course, that Judah was outrageously afraid but had decided not to let Jennifer see his fear. He had nearly mastered the art of hiding his true feelings and this little dance he was doing proved that—even if it was only to himself.

Eventually, the lunch was made and they piled two trays with food and another tray with dishes, glasses, napkins, and whatnot and so forth. "Judah, we forgot to make the drink." She was reminded of the last time she had made the drink for the group. It turned out that what she had concocted was some sort of poisonous liquid that Pierce wasted no time in pointing out, embarrassing her completely. Just as she opened her mouth again to ask what they should make, Bella popped through the entranceway. She had apparently heard the question, since she offered an answer.

"I'll make the drink," she said and then as though she had read Jennifer's thoughts, added, "we don't want to be poisoned now, do we." Bella chuckled and pinched Jennifer's arm teasingly.

"Not funny, Auntie," Jennifer replied, but a grin did crawl onto her face. She immediately chased it away.

"I'll finish up here and bring down this last tray," Bella said. "We're ready to eat, so let's get moving."

Judah picked up one tray and Jennifer scooped up the other. "Whoever designed this crazy hollow did a poor job," she said. "It's much too far between the kitchen and the eating stump." Jennifer sighed and disappeared into the passageway, counting on the lanterns to cast her and her brother some light.

"Don't wait for me, but save me some food," Bella hollered after them. "I'll be there shortly; I need to make up lunches for tomorrow."

"OK," the twins hollered at the same time.

Even though this passageway was now familiar to Jennifer, she was not yet comfortable in it. The lanterns were faithful to cast their light for her feet to move and her eyes to see, and it was nice and big—nothing like the other dark, cramped one she'd been in earlier. Still, she didn't feel safe. Judah was right behind her, but that's what she had thought in the other passageway when his hand —or what she'd thought had been his hand—was on her back.

As her mind replayed those events, she could almost feel that same hand again. *Jennifer, you are acting ridiculous*, she told herself. *Judah is behind me because I can hear the dishes on his tray clanging and banging. If he noticed anything unusual, he'd tell me. He would notice in this passageway because even though it's a bit shadowy, the lanterns are doing their job.*

Yes, it's light enough in here for Judah to see. And furthermore, she continued to rationalize with herself, *even though the lanterns don't cast light behind me, they will cast it in front of Judah. Since he's following me, Judah's "in front" is my "just behind," so he won't miss a thing.*

Her reasoning went on and on and on like Mr. Hall's English class back in fourth grade—that is, until her reasonings were interrupted by Simeon's truths. The moment Jennifer heard his voice echoing in her mind, she recognized her Shailma. She had not heard his voice for far too long—since he'd dropped her off at the hollow, in fact.

That WAS much too long. She wanted to ask him why he hadn't helped her in the cold passageway, but his powerful words now filled her thoughts, pushing the questions she had for him right back to the corner where they would remain unasked.

Jennifer, you cannot always count on someone else to see or hear or know such things. The being that touched your back in the narrow passageway does not have a body, as you know a body to be. Judah could not possibly have seen it, so he could not have warned you. Such bodiless beings are everywhere. They are invisible beings of the air and you cannot see them now. But as you fine tune the eyes of your heart, you will be able to see them, even if no one else can.

You have no need to fear them, for they hold no power over you. They exist here in Trilleah for the purpose of distracting you. Their tactics are to lie to you and cause you so much fear that you'll never return. Lies are all they have with which to taunt you. They belong to King Shrailzhar. Have no fear, Little One.

"WHAT?" Jennifer thought she was responding to Simeon in her mind, but when she heard Judah's voice responding, she knew she'd let her thoughts slip out and roll off of her tongue. She had no time to explain, however, and even if she did, Jennifer wasn't sure how she could explain such things. Just then, the passageway ended and she stepped into the light of the Eating Chamber.

Everyone was distracted and busy with their regular preparations. Pierce was rifling through maps, unfolding, looking puzzled, refolding. Matt was off in the far corner wrapping some odd things in dark brown leather strips. Sam was … well, who knows what it is that Sam does. And Miriam, well, she was nowhere to be found … as usual.

Jennifer and Judah set the trays on the eating stump, alerting everyone to the fact that their food had arrived.

"I hope you won't try to poison us this time," Pierce said. He had a smirk, but nonetheless, Jennifer was annoyed.

"Shut up, Pierce," she sneered. Her mind was whizzing today, and she had no time for his stupid remarks—teasing or not.

"Come and eat, everyone," Judah hollered loudly, since it was still unclear where Miriam may have been.

As they gathered around the eating stump, grabbing food and mercilessly teasing Jennifer about being poisoned, her mind was far from this place. What did Simeon mean, *they lie to you?* How could they lie to her? Could they give her their thoughts? How would she knew their thoughts from Simeon's … or from her own for that matter.

Around and around and around she went in her wonderings, spinning out of control and nearly driving herself mad. She was afraid they WOULD drive her mad, in fact, which only added to the spinning and twisting that was going on inside of her.

"Judah," she whispered so quietly that Jennifer wasn't sure he heard her. "I need to talk to you before you go to your Chamber."

Judah, being a very smart young man, knew Jennifer well. He knew not to ask her questions now; it was evident she did not wish to let anyone know that something was on her mind. He didn't say a word in reply. Instead, he nodded his head, let his elbow bang gently into hers, and made a low "mhm," sound, just to let her know that he had, indeed, heard her request.

Finally, with not much food left on the trays, Bella appeared with a large bag, wrapped and ready for tomorrow's journey. She set it by the row of cloaks and moved toward the stump. "Hey, you guys didn't save me much," she teased, but plenty of food remained for her tiny appetite.

Bella squeezed into where Sam had just exited from and filled her plate with bits of this and morsels of that. She began chattering on about the journey, what still needed to be done to get ready, and started talking with Pierce about the maps. Everyone else seemed to be lighthearted and chitter-chattering about nothing significant whatsoever.

Jennifer's mind was elsewhere, though, somewhere surely no one else's mind would be and a place where she wished that she could pull her mind away from, for indeed, it was a place she did not want to be either. Nevertheless, there she was.

If each could see into the other's minds, they would all see the same thing. Fear … dread … panic … exhaustion. There was no real lightheartedness whatsoever, not even a trace, in any of them. Most put on a good show, though, convincing the others they were unconcerned about tomorrow's journey.

To know this might have caused Jennifer's soul some slivers of calmness but unfortunately, she had no way of knowing such things. Each was so preoccupied with trying to convince the others of their braveness (and perhaps trying to convince themselves as well), that none considered sharing the truth about their anxious fears. No one considered that such truths may prove to be quite helpful to the others, so no one let their thoughts be known by anyone else.

Perhaps they should have.

Altogether Unexplainable

chapter eighteen

It would have helped Jennifer. Especially right now when she thought she was the only one who was full of dread. *Why am I here?* she wondered, so completely absorbed in her thoughts that she tuned out the rest of the conversation around her.

I'm not brave like the rest, her thoughts meandered. *I don't see well with the eyes of my heart. I don't know anything about the land. I don't even know about this hollow—this place of so-called safety. It doesn't seem all that safe to me.*

She was getting herself so worked up that her hands were beginning to sweat, so she picked up the soft blue napkin—still unused—from beside her plate. Without realizing it, her fingers began rolling the corners and tearing bits off. Before long, she had reduced the napkin to a pile of blue fluff and without noticing, everyone had started watching her. They weren't sure whether to giggle in their nervousness or be concerned with Jennifer's distractedness. After all, distractedness was a dangerous thing in the land of Trilleah.

Judah noticed and put his much bigger hand over his sister's tiny one to get her attention. "I think we should clean up this mess and get some rest." His words distracted everyone away from Jennifer. Instantly chairs began squawking as they were pushed back on the dirt floor, and meaningless chatter started again with Bella rattling an endless list of instructions to the others.

"Matt, if you pile the dishes up and take them to the kitchen, Sam you can go with him and begin cleaning up this mess, please." When Bella gave instructions, it was in such a way that no one ever felt like she was being bossy. She was so kind and matter-of-fact about it all that it seemed the natural order of things. People went about doing whatever it was Bella had instructed them to. She was genuinely a wonderful person, and everyone loved her; everyone, it seemed, except Miriam.

Miriam was either jealous of—or annoyed by—Bella most of the time. Bella felt the same way toward Miriam. From the second they had met in Malleana Forest, Bella felt threatened by Miriam but had not been able to figure out why. That made it even worse. Maybe if Bella had understood why those feelings arose within her it might have helped, but then again, maybe it would not have helped at all. Bella wasn't sure about that. The one thing she was sure of was that there was something distressing about this black-haired, pale-skinned girl who had come to Trilleah.

None of that seemed important right now. As everyone was busily carrying out Bella's instructions, Jennifer thought it a good time to grab Judah and sneak away to have that badly needed conversation. She hung around the table a bit longer than everyone else, and when Matt had finally gathered all the dishes and walked toward the entranceway to the kitchen, Judah moved back to the eating stump.

"Judah," she whispered.

"Jennifer, I'm going to go through the passageway toward the kitchen. Do you know the secret chamber just inside? The one by the tiny bench a few steps to the left?"

Jennifer screwed up her face as she thought for a second, but then remembered her first trip down that entranceway. She had been running with a picture of Mamma and Daddy when she'd tripped, breaking the picture frame, and Bella had shown her the bench and how it wasn't a bench at all but rather a hidden doorway to a secret chamber. "I know where it is," she whispered.

"Give me a five-minute head start and then meet me there," Judah whispered. "I'll wait for you." He didn't wait for her to respond before he sauntered through the entranceway.

He's brilliant, was Jennifer's first thought. Nobody would suspect they were going off to have a secret meeting down that entranceway. If her first thought was full of confidence in her brother, her second thought was completely the opposite.

Had Judah ever been in that chamber? How did he know there was nothing odd or threatening behind the secret entrance? Or did he know? Did he even think to consider such a thing?

Up until just a bit ago, Jennifer thought—as did everyone else—that the entire hollow was safe. She had recently learned that it wasn't safe after all, and she needed to be much more cautious and aware of her surroundings. She'd learned that there were beings invisible to the eye in this hollow. Was there only that one? She doubted it, for if one unseen creature could get in, surely they could all get in. Jennifer remembered that Simeon had told her they were everywhere and suddenly, her mind churned a little too quickly for her own good. No longer did she wish to meet Judah, or anyone else for that matter, in any unknown passageways or chambers.

Jennifer thought about it awhile and finally decided that she couldn't leave Judah there waiting; she really did need to speak to him. She didn't realize that Judah had invited Bella to their secret meeting. Consequently, when Jennifer caught sight of her auntie darting into the passageway it never crossed her mind to consider where she might be heading.

In just another minute or two, Jennifer walked quietly to the same entranceway that everyone else seemed to be wandering through and headed toward the bench. Once there, she looked around. When Jennifer saw no one, she bent down and lifted the lid expecting, but surprised nevertheless, a small door to appear in the wall.

She stepped in and looked around. A few Solstice journeys before this one, when Bella had shown her how the bench worked, Jennifer had only noticed the small secret door. She never looked inside nor wondered about it again.

But now as she stepped inside, she gasped. Her eyes grew into large pools as they drank in all there was to see in such a well-hidden space. It was nearly unbelievable, in fact, and she wondered why they didn't meet here, inside this chamber, more often.

Jennifer's eyes moved carefully from left to right as she scanned the space, trying to take it all in and make some sense of it which, of course, couldn't be done. The space was enormous; much larger than the Eating Chamber they spent most of their time squished into … and the light! There were no lanterns here—at least none that she could find. The light seemed to be clear, *altogether unexplainable*, she thought. It was well lit even though she could not find any source of light, but it wasn't what one would especially call "bright." The only possible word she could locate in all her known words to describe such an indescribable light was "pure." The light was so pure it removed any shadows that might have otherwise remained.

She tried to find a dark corner here or a shadow there but could locate neither. Each nook and every cranny seemed to have just as much light as anywhere else. There were no deep, hidden crevices or dim spots where the pure light failed to be. The unsourced light seemed to have the slightest shade of blue lingering throughout, but when Jennifer tried to see blue, she couldn't separate it from the light. *Altogether unexplainable*, she thought again. In fact, *altogether unexplainable*, were the only words that she could think of at all inside of this hidden chamber.

There were no pictures on the walls in this secret space, yet somehow the walls themselves formed mesmerizing masterpieces. The rock walls, while similar to the rest of the rock walls she'd seen in the Eating Chamber or the Cooking Chamber or even her own Sleeping Chamber, were somehow different. They were rock, yes, but there seemed to be formed within them, bewildering designs and brilliant colors and endless patterns. They danced and shone in the clear blue light. Nothing any human hand had formed could be found and any masterpieces their eyes did see were created within the walls themselves; intricate designs created by the hard rocky surfaces.

Altogether unexplainable, she thought again, mouthing the words. Her eyes were as big as saucers, taking it all in; absorbing it fully.

There was not much furniture to take notice of. No tree stumps were poking through the dirt floor, although, there was a small ice box on one side with what looked like a rock jutting in from the side wall.

There was no particular washroom either. However, something told Jennifer that there might be a secret door somewhere which might lead to a toilet. This chamber looked very much like it would be a place to come if one needed to hide out for a long time, although the icebox certainly would not hold much.

While the entire space was breathtakingly stunning, what astonished her beyond words was the deep, red-colored-yet-translucent rocks. Everywhere she looked, there they were. Gigantic. Brilliant. The reddest reds she'd ever seen. Next, her eyes landed on some similar rock-looking structures with different colors. The blues were like an ocean, but one that made you crave a drink—clear and shimmering. The reds were deep and thick, yet not thick enough to make them solid. There were amber rocks and green rocks … oh, those greens. They were like the most luscious grass one's eyes might ever hope to see.

Never had her eyes beheld such colors, yet her mind could make no sense of the clearness of them; thick yet translucent. If she'd not seen it with her own eyes, she most certainly wouldn't have believed it. She barely believed anyway, even while her own eyes worked hard to inhale it all.

There was only one word to describe this altogether indescribable chamber. It was what made her want to remain tucked inside its walls for all time and never go back to the passageway, or the Eating Chamber, or her little space in the hollow, or even to the little house nestled quietly on the corner of Viewmont Lane and Mitchell Avenue.

It was pure and unfiltered.

It was exquisitely intoxicating.

It was light and glorious.

It was *peace*.

Hidden Chambers

chapter nineteen

Yes, that was the word; peace. The moment Jennifer stepped into this space, an overwhelming peace filled her from the bottom of her feet to the very top of her head. Every cell in her body opened up and absorbed the peace in a full measure.

Her breaths seemed pure. Her mind was at rest—something she'd not experienced since her parents' accident. Her skin felt clear, somehow translucent—as if someone may be able to see right into her soul. In this place, at this moment, someone seeing into her soul would have been perfectly OK because suddenly Jennifer had nothing to hide, nothing to fear, nothing to dread, no questions to ask, no explanations to search for. Peace was the only thing she felt or thought. It filled her insides and swaddled her outsides.

"You wanted to talk to me, Jelly Bean?" The familiar voice of her twin brother wafted through the air and tickled her ears. She had no recollection of why it was that she'd asked to talk with him. Jennifer did not wish to disrupt the air with words, so she nodded her head, not even glancing in the direction of Judah.

She closed her eyes and let the purity of this space flood in and exist in her body, content and fully alive. She'd not felt this alive since, well, ever, she supposed. The longer she remained, the longer she wanted to remain. Trilleah, the Forest of Malleana, even her little yellow house tucked quietly on the corner of Viewmont Lane and Mitchell Avenue, could do without her.

"J," she heard Bella whisper. Rather than respond, Jennifer took a deeper breath. Whatever was in this room was cleansing all the darkness, all the fear, all the doubt of herself and the situation, from her soul. All those things were being replaced with a consuming light, an overwhelming peace, and a fullness of confidence not in herself, but in something much bigger than herself.

If she remained in this spot for the rest of time, it would not have been long enough.

"J," she heard Bella say again. "Isn't it magical? Just being in this space transforms your soul."

"Mhm," was all Jennifer uttered in return.

"We can't stay," Bella said. Those words should have brought much disappointment, but even they were wrapped in peace. It was as if all other emotion faded away in this space and had to wait outside the door. Finally, Jennifer decided to speak, but what she'd been feeling earlier, back in the Eating Chamber, did not become the basis of her words.

"Why don't we spend more time here?" she sincerely asked.

"Because the more time you are here, the harder it is to leave," Bella answered.

"And," Judah added, "as brilliant as it would be to remain here for all of time, we cannot. We won't find any clay tablets in this Chamber."

Jennifer's mind would usually want to argue or at least ask a hundred questions. But here, in this place, no more questions came to her mind. She felt no need to argue as she normally would. So that was that. The three of them remained in the perfect space, drinking in all the peace that was available, and it seemed there was an endless supply.

Finally, after what was not enough time, Bella lifted a small bench seat and the secret door opened.

"It's time to go," she whispered and quickly darted back into the dimly lit passageway. What was odd—odder than all the things Jennifer had just felt, seen, and experienced—was that even though she wanted to feel sad about having to leave, Jennifer could not locate that particular feeling anywhere.

So, like Bella, she too slipped through the small door hidden in the rocks; Judah exited right behind her. The moment they were standing back in the passageway, the door shut itself up and the most magnificent Chamber became invisible to them once more.

"What … was … THAT?" Jennifer finally asked after the three of them had stood quietly in the passageway for a number of moments.

"That, my dear J, was the Chamber of Rest," Bella whispered, trying to hold onto and savor every morsel she'd feasted on inside its walls.

"It's the best place ever," Judah sighed. "It's like no place else. I dread going in only because I know I'll have to come back out. Jennifer, you'll find now that you've experienced the Chamber of Rest that no other place will satisfy you. The shadows will seem a little more shadowy; the passageways will appear a bit dimmer and the unrest will be a bit more restless."

Judah and Bella sighed loudly, remembering the feeling the Chamber of Rest had given them.

The twins would have been perfectly happy to remain in the dimly lit passageway for the remainder of their time in Trilleah. Bella however, always the wise and strong leader, knew differently.

"We need to get some rest for tomorrow. Even though our

souls are in complete rest from the Chamber, our bodies need sleep. You two go off to bed now. Morning is going to come much too soon." The words came from Bella as she pointed with one hand toward their Sleeping Chambers and with the other toward the Eating Chamber. "I'm going to check on the others. I hope I find them all gone to their Chambers, but I doubt that very much."

Except for Matt, nobody else could ever seem to do what they knew they should be doing without Bella's constant watchful eye and continual directions. Jennifer found herself wondering about this a lot, but now was not one of those times. For this moment, all she could think of was where she'd just been. Judah interrupted her dreamy thoughts.

"Jelly Bean, Bella's right. I don't know what time it is, but I do know that when one is in the Chamber of Rest, time races by faster than it seems."

"We were only in there for a few minutes, Judah," Jennifer protested.

Judah looked down at his watch and chuckled. "Yes, just like I thought," he said to her. "We were in there for nearly an hour and a half," he said, turning his watch toward his sister so she could see for herself. Judah knew she'd not believe him otherwise.

"What?" she gasped. "No, that can't be," and she grabbed Judah's wrist, turning his arm slightly so that she could see the time. "I can't believe it, Judah!" she exclaimed and began laughing. "Well, I'm off to my Sleeping Chamber then."

They both walked down the passageway in silence until Jennifer reached her Chamber. "Good night, Judah," she said. She slipped her foot into the small hole and for the first time was not surprised when the door opened up to her, welcoming her in.

"Good night, Jelly Bean," Judah echoed and continued down the passageway to his own secret door.

Meanwhile back in the Eating Chamber, Bella was pleasantly surprised to find it empty. She was less pleasant and less surprised to find many of the dishes still sitting on the loaded trays on the eating stump. However, Bella rarely got annoyed and because she was full of such peace at this moment, she was even less likely to have any poor thoughts. She picked up the tray and turned to go back down the passageway.

"Here we go," she said, smiling brightly.

"Here we go," a peculiar and barely noticeable voice echoed back. Bella was so lost in her pleasant thoughts that her mind barely heard the echo. In fact, it was only heard in the deepest underlying place of her soul. Rather than demanding to be heard, the words tucked themselves away to be retrieved and remembered later and remind Bella that they had been heard at all.

The time for sleep passed quickly and while some may have slept rather poorly, Judah, Jennifer, and Bella slept more soundly than they could even speak of.

After being in the Chamber of Rest, everything seemed a bit different. Each of them knew it would only last a short time. It would, however, give them the courage to complete their journey, or at least, that was their hope as they each drifted soundly into the sweetest of sleep.

Dreary Day of Dread

chapter twenty

Each time one entered the Chamber of Rest, the feelings they experienced lasted a bit longer than the time before. But each time, that sharpness and the overcoming rest would eventually be replaced with the usual fear, anxiousness, and uncertainty that accompanied them like old friends on these dark and dangerous journeys.

Now, one by one, they gathered in the Eating Chamber with their cloaks draped over their arms and the death gray boots, as

Jennifer referred to them, fastened firmly to their feet. Bella, not yet in sight, had obviously already been there and had delivered large trays filled with blueberry muffins, juice, hot chocolate, and a large steaming pot of oatmeal. It looked delicious and smelled even better.

As they arrived one by one, they began digging into the feast that had been prepared for them. Jennifer picked up a knife and skimmed a generous amount of butter off the top of the block. She spread it on a muffin and opened her mouth wide, taking a bite so big she nearly choked. Sam could not miss such an opportunity and laughed loudly, making some lame remark that nobody but Jennifer heard … and ignored.

In the same moment, Bella returned to the Eating Chamber with many large bags. She set them by the empty hooks that typically held the cloaks, and cleared her throat. "I made a bag for each of you so, please … PLEASE remember to take the one with your name on it when we leave the hollow. Which, by the way, we must do soon."

A little more of the peace that was still lingering in the twins' souls escaped. "Awww," fluttered out from between Jennifer's lips as she felt the peace quickly being replaced with more common feelings that she was beginning to get used to; dread, sorrow, anxiousness, fear.

"Bella," Matt called as she again darted into the dimness of the passageway. "You'd better come eat before it's gone." She popped her head back into the chamber.

"Thanks, Matt. I ate earlier," she said, and then, was gone again.

There was very little chatter among the Travelers as they finished every morsel of food on the table. As one plate emptied, someone would set it on the tray, another would stack on top of that one, and another would wobble on top of the growing pile. Soon, even the crumbs were gobbled up and all the dishes were back on the trays—where they would remain until the Travelers returned later tonight.

As if right on cue, Bella appeared, glanced toward the table, and grinned in satisfaction. "OK, let's get going." She nodded toward the door and swung a cloak around her shoulders. Before she disappeared inside the hood, she reminded everyone to grab the bags she'd set out earlier.

Miriam stooped down and picked up the bag with her name scribbled across the top. It was by far the smallest of all the bags and she seemed to feel it was cause for complaint. "I don't know what this is about, but it would seem mine's very tiny. Since we have to carry them all day, I suppose I'm glad."

Judah picked his up which was quite heavy. "Want to trade, Miriam?" he asked. "I'll carry yours if you carry mine!" He held his arm out toward Miriam, who ignored him and tucked her bag inside of the cloak.

"Judah," Matt interrupted the bag carrying fiasco. "The cloaks have pockets inside to carry things. No matter how heavy the 'thing' is, if you stick it into one of the pockets, the cloak absorbs the weight; you won't even notice it." Matt laughed loudly. "Have you never noticed all the things Bella randomly pulls from her cloak?" Now Pierce decided that since fun was being made of some of the Travelers, it would be the perfect time for him to jump into the conversation.

"Where do you think she carried all that stuff?" Pierce laughed, but it was not a kind laugh—not like the one that came from Matt. Pierce had such a nasty way to him and at that moment, the very last remaining bits of peace from the Chamber of Rest escaped from both Judah and Jennifer.

Now Jennifer, always one to come to Judah's defense whether he needed her to or not, opened her mouth to say something much too nasty back to Pierce when Bella's voice rang out instead. "OK you guys, hush! Enough of this nonsense. For whoever may not know," she said, sounding quite agitated, "if you feel around inside of your cloak, you'll find what seems like a pocket. I don't know how, I didn't create them, but you can put whatever you need in the pockets and the pockets will do the carrying for you. You'll not feel anything at all, no matter the size of the bag or the weight of the items."

"Furthermore," she pulled her hood down and sounded more perturbed than before, likely because of Miriam's whining more than any other reason. "What's in your bags is essential for this journey. I had my reasons for splitting the items up as I did, so please keep all whining to yourself, since your cloak will be taking the weight of the bags."

With that, she disappeared under the grayness of the hood and with one small step, the secret door to the hollow opened. One by one, they stooped down to pick up their bags, stuffed them into the pockets inside the cloaks, pulled up their hoods, and stepped into the openness—and dullness—of Trilleah. The sky seemed especially dark this morning. Of course, it was always a shade of bleak gray here in the land, but then again, they had never left the safety of the hollow quite so early before.

There was an unusual hum in the air, one not heard before. It seemed to have a bit of a pounding to it; a heartbeat, maybe. The sound was so distant that the Travelers could easily miss it, yet at the same time, it surrounded them. In and out, in and out it went— like the air itself was breathing, as though the land had a heartbeat all its own. It would have been difficult to explain if anyone had tried, which of course, nobody did. Nevertheless, their bellies told them something had changed in the dark land since their last journey through the Fowler's Snare.

The king knows you're here, the familiar voice whispered inside Jennifer's troubled mind. *His armies have been waiting for you,* the calm voice of Simeon reminded her. *This is what you're hearing.*

That cannot lead to anything good, she thought back.

Nothing in this land of traps, snares, and lies is of any good, Jennifer, not one thing. But you are correct. This is one of the most, "not good things" of all the possible "not good things" you could face. Shrailzhar is looking and he has his armies looking. Even his shadows are prowling around looking for your souls to devour like a hungry lion on this dreariest of days.

Simeon was usually so calming and reassuring to Jennifer that she wondered if this voice was his at all. He was bringing many things this dark morning, but reassurance was not one of them. Fear and dread? Absolutely—in triplicate!

Jennifer assumed that every trace of peace she'd captured in the Chamber of Rest was long gone by now. Nevertheless, Simeon suggested she look deeper.

Go to the Chamber of Rest in your mind, Little One. That seemed an odd thought, but she did her best to obey. In the very deepest place of her mind, where she'd carefully hidden the moments from her short time in the Chamber of Rest, she now went back to search for them.

In her mind's eye, she could see the brilliant reds, magnificent blues, and luscious greens of the large rocks and the detailed patterns woven into the walls. For a moment the feelings of peace were gently stirred and somehow, a warrior spirit arose within this small-framed, timid, young girl. She knew that whatever was to come on this dark day, she would somehow find the courage to keep going. Brave or not so brave, she vowed to continue the journey; no matter what.

With everyone tucked away inside their dark coverings and dingy boots, it was lonely in Trilleah. Inside the hollow such wonderful things happened, but the very instant they stepped through the hidden entrance and into the dark land, all wonderful things ceased to exist.

As Jennifer's mind wandered around and around, she was not paying attention to where her feet were going. She finally realized they'd been going in a direction they had not gone before. Every other journey began by heading straight—out the hollow and straight to the caves where they could lay out the Living Maps.

This time, however, Jennifer noticed they had circled the hollow and were going in the opposite direction. In fact, as Jennifer took a rest from her swirling mind, she saw they were going straight through the Malleana Forest.

How very odd, she told herself.

As usual, when she did not know something she couldn't simply let it go and trust that whoever was leading this pack of wanderers knew where they were going. Her mind began swirling faster and she made her feet speed up. She hoped to find either Bella or Judah. Where was Judah?

Oh dear. It was impossible to tell one from another in this group of cloak-covered Travelers.

Something arose from within Jennifer's belly and the thought weaved its way through her mind until it found a home right in the center of her heart.

Are you sure these are the same ones you left the hollow with, little girl?

Jennifer looked around, trying to peak outside of her hood. "Where did THAT come from?" she whispered. Now she moved even faster and didn't care which of the Travelers she found, as long as the face she saw buried in the hood was a familiar one. She was beginning to wonder if she wanted to see the faces of anyone in those hoods. *What if they aren't who I left the hollow with? What if I don't recognize any of them? What if ...*

On and on her mind wandered, completely unrestrained and unguarded. But as Jennifer would soon learn the hard way, keeping one's mind guarded and under control was a good idea; a very good idea indeed.

Coals of Fire

twenty one

Catching up with whoever was immediately in front of her, Jennifer spun herself around and glared up into the hood. She found the kind face of Matt gazing back at her. He was deeply thoughtful and didn't even notice her odd behavior. He nodded and took her by the hand.

Leave it to Matt, she thought. *He always knows how to calm my soul without ever knowing it was anxious.*

They continued to walk together; Jennifer found herself pondering why the presence of someone she could see with her eyes was so much more calming than the presence of the Shailmas which, of course, she could not see. Even though she'd experienced their power and wisdom, and even after she'd had many conversations with Simeon and had seen him in the portal between her little yellow house and the Solstice Gate, she still had the hardest of times trusting in him when her eyes could not see him. *If I could only see you*, she thought of her dear Simeon, *I'd be at rest.*

Jennifer, you know I am here with you. All at once the thoughts of Simeon flooded her mind. *It's of utmost importance that you begin to believe—even when you cannot see. Just believe, Little One. Just Believe.* She was getting more and more frustrated with his one constant request and told him so.

How can I believe when I don't see? she asked, genuinely wanting an answer. *Simeon, how badly I want to trust you. I do! But it's so hard. Help me.*

My dear Little One, Simeon said compassionately in her mind. *I do realize this is a great difficulty. I never told you it would be easy, only that it would be necessary and possible. All things are possible when you believe.*

Then show me how; help me. Jennifer's tone was softening, even if the words were unspoken. She did want to know how to trust something she could neither see nor feel nor touch. She had seen the great power of the Shailmas when they left her little house and entered into Trilleah only hours earlier. If she'd seen that power then, felt that safety then, why did it escape her now? Somehow she must make herself believe. The harder she tried, the more disappointed she became.

Jennifer felt Matt squeeze her hand and she smiled, unaware that he was trying to get her attention so that she would notice what was surrounding them on the path. Instead, she nodded and continued her silent conversation with Simeon, ignoring what she should have been paying attention to.

The conversation ended quickly as Matt shoved the distracted girl behind him. If she'd seen what he was seeing, Jennifer would have been more than grateful for his yanking on her arm. But she had not seen and so instead, was offended by Matt's gesture.

She jerked her hand out of his and slowed a bit, falling behind him; far enough behind for Judah to stumble into her. He grabbed her by the cloak just as she tumbled toward the ground. Now she was even more irritated and becoming angry.

She was about ready to turn and tell Judah off—then Matt— but as her mouth opened, so did her eyes. What she saw were creatures … many creatures. Some were behind this tree, others behind that one; the more trees she looked at the more creatures she saw peering out from around them. They were everywhere in the forest—watching the Travelers and chattering to one another using clicking and ticks to communicate.

Oh, why had they come this way, she demanded to know but of course, no one offered an answer, since the question was a silent one.

Keep yourself calm, she heard Simeon whisper in the shadows of her mind. *Do not grow weary for shortly you will be through the forest to the other side and these creatures cannot exist for long outside of the forest.*

Keep calm? Are you JOKING? It seemed that his request was anything but reasonable. With hundreds of hollow black eyes staring at her, watching her every step, how was she supposed to remain calm? An unthinkable task! Completely undoable. *I cannot do this Simeon. I cannot.*

No, by yourself you cannot. Jennifer, look at me. Do not look to the right. Do not look to the left. Do not look at the creatures. Do not let your eyes wander into the darkness. Keep your eyes focused on me and we shall get through. Trust me, Little One. Trust me. Simeon's words sounded great but they seemed unreasonable.

She felt something beside her foot, then again and again and again. Jennifer hung back and waited for Judah to move up beside her. With no words spoken, she reached her hand out slightly and in the way only a twin could do, Judah did the same.

Their hands found one another and their fingers entwined tightly together. Jennifer had hoped she'd find courage and strength through her brother's hand, but all she found was sweaty fear.

Adding his fear to her own was nearly crippling and she felt her knees begin to weaken and wobble.

As something continued to bump into her feet, she looked down to see fireballs. One after another after another, what looked like fist-sized balls of fire—burning coals perhaps—were landing on the ground around their feet. *What is this?* she shrieked in her mind. Oh, how she wished Judah could hear her thoughts. If only she could stir up enough confidence in her Shailma, it would somehow seem a bit better.

The burdensome cloaks were not hiding the Travelers from whatever these fireball-throwing-black-eyed-creatures were. It seemed, though, that while the creatures could see them and fling flaming coals at them, they were afraid of the Travelers. At least, this was the reasoning in Jennifer's mind. Surely if they were not afraid of the Travelers, they'd not be hiding behind the cursed trees.

As all her reasoning and thinking and panic wove themselves not so neatly together, Jennifer suddenly knew the truth. *THEY ARE TROWS!* As the reality of the creatures' identity flooded her, she had to force herself not to throw up. Terror raced through her veins, causing her skin to become cold and her stomach uneasy. These creatures were the very ones who'd stolen her mother's soul. Then came a thought a thousand times worse. *They are trying to steal OUR souls ...*

The near silence of the forest was painful. How the Travelers' ears longed to hear something—anything—other than the sound of the fiery darts that were thump, thump, thumping against their cloaks and falling with a thud to the ground. The Trows themselves made no sound. The trees, typically echoing painful groans, were also noticeably silent.

The stifled breaths wafting within their hoods were the only sounds to be heard as they escaped through quivering lips. Jennifer, still with her hand locked firmly in Judah's, was as cold as ice. She dared not look to the right or the left but instead focused on keeping her eyes staring straight ahead, much too afraid to make eye contact with one of these shadowy demons lest it somehow capture her soul with just a glance. Never had she been so scared that she couldn't form a thought. But even those, it seemed, had hidden behind dark corners in her mind and had become silent.

Judah pulled his sister as close to himself as he could but not so close that they would trip over each other. Jennifer had no way of knowing for sure, but if she could have read Judah's thoughts or seen a glimpse of his face, it would have confirmed he was just as afraid as she.

A very few but torturous moments passed.

Moving carefully together, Judah and Jennifer stepped quicker and moved closer to Matt and Sam, who'd been walking ahead of them. At about the same time, they felt whoever was behind them move closer as well. Being sandwiched between the other Travelers, the twins felt only a hair less afraid.

If they could see what the Trows saw, however, they'd have not been afraid at all. As the Trows peered out from behind their many hiding places in the Forest of Waiting Ones, it appeared to their evil eyes that the Travelers had somehow managed to meld themselves together into one giant gray being. Even greater still, and terrifyingly troublesome to the beastly Trows, was what had moved in to surround the Travelers. It certainly was not the Travelers that the Trows were afraid of, for Travelers, even tightly knit together as one, were no match for a forest full of evil Trows.

Unseen to any eyes but the Trows, a great and mighty army of Shamar Shailmas had moved in and was now moving along with the Travelers. Too many to count, the Shailmas were enormous, and each was covered in solid, silver armor.

It was these Shailmas who'd caused the fiery darts to fall to the ground; it was they who stepped on the flaming coals, extinguishing them before they could harm the Travelers, allowing themselves to be burned instead. It was the Shamar Shailmas that caused the Trows to stay mostly hidden behind the trees.

It was the Shailmas.

Like a Mouse to Cheese

Suddenly, and without warning, the arrows stopped and the trees again began their heavy moaning. Heartbreaking as the sound was, the Travelers would later agree it was better than no sound at all. So, the groaning continued and the Travelers breathed a bit lighter for the time being as they came to the far edge of the forest where the Solstice Gates sat, still open and waiting for the sun to return to its place somewhere beyond the horizon.

Finally out of Malleana Forest where the souls of the Waiting Ones groaned and the Trows awaited a more opportune time with the Travelers, someone felt free to speak … the one someone who probably shouldn't have spoken at all.

"Who decided that this was the way we should come?" Miriam demanded to know, apparently unhappy with such a decision and angry with whoever had made it. She stopped abruptly, causing everyone to bump into each other and spun around to face the group. "Who decided?" she demanded again, her tone impatient and rather ugly.

"I decided!" Pierce replied sharply. "I made that decision because before any of you were in the Eating Chamber this morning, I had the Living Maps laid out on the stump." He crossed his arms as if scolding a small child. "I read the maps carefully, over and over and over again. When it was clear this was the direction the path was taking, I asked Bella to double check. She did."

Bella stepped up and immediately came to Pierce's defense. "Yes, that's the truth. Pierce was very disturbed at what the maps were suggesting so he had me double check and indeed, the unseen finger drew a path straight through Malleana Forest. Neither of us liked it, but we have learned to always follow the map's direction … always."

"If you have a problem with that, I'd suggest you deal with it yourself because you were certainly not there to read the maps, Miriam." Bella's voice was getting louder and louder, something quite unusual for her, at least outside of the hollow, but something that was becoming more common with the constant annoyances from Miriam. Pierce, too, noticed Bella's rising anger and put his hand on her shoulder in an attempt to calm her before things got out of control.

"It doesn't matter who decided or who's angry about it," Judah joined the conversation, trying to distract the rising tension between Miriam and Bella. He'd always been a peacemaker whenever he saw the need to do so. He was also good at pointing out the obvious and bringing common sense to an otherwise senseless situation.

Maybe he had developed this skill because he had a sister who so often lacked any sense at all. Jennifer would have laughed at such a thought if she weren't so dumbfounded with all the goings-on. It was bad enough having just come through an altogether terrifying place in Trilleah, but seeing Bella get immediately worked up by Miriam was equally unsettling.

Judah continued. "The fact is that we did go through the forest; we made it through and now we are here, out of the forest, and we need to keep going." Everyone nodded and made sounds of "mhm," and "yes," and other things that sounded quite agreeable.

"I will lead us to where we need to get to; where the Living Maps showed me this morning," Pierce snarled. He looked straight at Miriam and added, "Does anyone have a problem with that?"

Miriam glared right back but kept quiet.

"OK then!" Pierce said and spun around, again beginning to lead the Travelers in a highly undesirable direction.

They walked and walked and walked. This turn, that turn, another turn left, one more right, back left again. It seemed as though the Travelers were going in an odd direction that was leading them nowhere. It was more like a pattern of nonsense than a path leading anywhere in particular.

There were tall, thick trees along both sides of them; trees crammed so close together that they formed what one might describe as a wall. There was not a great number of leaves, but it seemed that while they had escaped the Forest of Waiting Ones long ago, they'd entered another forest of some sort—a bit of a maze perhaps, that was drawing them into its core like a vacuum.

These trees were very different from the ones in Malleana Forest. In fact, they were different from anything they'd yet seen in Trilleah. Certainly, there were no spaces or holes between the trunks of these towering trees, where they could slip through and escape this path. They weren't rounded so that light could peek through but more square-like and crisscrossed together like bricks on a sidewalk.

Perhaps the trees wandered along with them. It did seem to the Travelers as though the trees forming these suffocating walls were beginning to look the same as just a few minutes ago, and again a few minutes before that. In fact, they were all starting to look the same. Before very long at all, that was all they could see.

Walls of trees to the right … walls of trees to the left … walls of trees before them … and if they were to try and turn back, yet another wall of the same trees stood at attention behind them. The farther they wandered into the path, the higher these walls of trees arose. There seemed to be no way back, so they continued moving ahead.

They may have thought Pierce took a wrong turn somewhere along the way, but so far there had been no other turns to choose. From the instant they stepped onto this path, it was the only path available. It was not as if at any point he could have chosen right instead of left or left rather than right. No, there had never been any choices in which way to turn, so they followed where the path took them. It was almost as if—no, that couldn't have been—but yet it was; as if the path was taking them exactly where it wanted them to go. Yes, the path was certainly the leader in this game of cat and mouse.

"It seems like we've been walking for hours," Sam whined.

"It does, indeed," Matt agreed.

"Me feet are blistered," Jennifer mumbled.

"We've been out here for too long. The first good resting spot we see," Bella said, "we'll stop and eat something. I don't know about everyone else, but I'm starving."

Others mumbled and complained as well, agreeing it must soon be time to stop. The day was passing quickly, and they didn't seem to be getting anywhere significant.

"Do you think it would be all right, Bella?" Jennifer asked as she pulled her cloak hood back just enough for her face to peer out and her words to be heard, "if we took our hoods down for a bit? I'm feeling muffled."

"I see no reason that it should cause a problem," Bella said.

Matt agreed. "We've seen no sign of anything in this maze that would suggest we need to keep them up. In fact," he screwed up his face and continued, sounding a bit puzzled, "we haven't heard any sounds at all since we left Malleana Forest."

"Creepy," Sam said, and he pulled his hood back. As soon as he did, his hair went completely crazy. The hood must have created some static, causing his already wild hair to spiral out of control. Jennifer burst out laughing as she pulled her hood off, wondering if maybe her long hair would do the same thing. It didn't.

"Oh Sam," she giggled and ran her hand over his head, trying to force a few strands to lay down.

One by one, the Travelers' faces appeared from within the confines of their hoods and one by one they breathed a little more freely and felt a little less panicked; except for Miriam. She kept her hood up and her face hidden. She certainly was a suspicious one and didn't even try to fit in with the others.

With their hoods down, their faces exposed, and their chatting unguarded, they became easy targets for whatever might be lurking … looking … waiting. They should not have let their guard down even for the smallest moment, however, for with each step they wandered deeper and deeper into the meticulously designed trap of the Labyrinth set by King Shrailzhar himself.

Perhaps it was because of the enormous tension growing in the group, or maybe the continual stress of traveling such difficult journeys was proving to be too much. Whatever the reason, and indeed the reason itself did not matter, the Travelers were so unguarded in their wanderings inside this perfectly planned maze that they failed to notice the stiff breeze that had begun to stir. If they had noticed, they surely would have heard the dark laughter riding on the wings of the wind.

The Travelers were not alone even though their eyes could see no one else accompanying them. Unknown to any of them, this maze was just that, yet so much more. It was a Labyrinth. It was an elaborate and perfectly set trap laid out specifically for them, drawing them in like a mouse to the cheese. While there was indeed only one way in, there was also only one way out. Unbeknown to the Travelers, however, those two paths were most certainly not the same.

Bit of a Blunder

Now, one would certainly think that if a maze, no matter how detailed or elaborate that maze may be, had only one way to the center, that one could simply turn around and retrace their steps and it would lead them right back out. Unfortunately, this is not the case with a perfidious Labyrinth.

What the Travelers were failing to notice was that as they would turn a corner, the path they'd just traveled would shift behind them. If they had turned around right at that moment, or any moment here in the Labyrinth, they'd have been shocked to find that the path they had just walked had closed itself off. But they did not turn around; not at any point. The path leading the Travelers in was altering itself right behind them, leaving no way out. At least, not a way out that would be readily accessible—if they could find it at all.

Another turn to the left and again to the right, a few steps forward and another turn, and another and another after that.

"Are we getting anywhere at all?" Sam whined.

"It doesn't seem like it," Pierce replied. "Bella," Pierce continued, "we've got to stop. We need to recheck the maps."

"No kidding we need to recheck the maps!" The sharp, venomous words exploded from Miriam's mouth. The look on her barely exposed face showed that even she was surprised by her boldness. The look that smeared across her face suggested that she'd never intended for her words to be spoken out loud; she bit her lip. Pierce glared at her and then looked away, ignoring her.

"Besides, Bella, I think we need to eat something. I'm starving." Bella nodded to Pierce and pointed to a slightly wider spot just ahead, where it seemed that an intersection might finally emerge. It looked, for the first time since they'd entered this maze, like they would get to make a choice on which way to go.

"Seems like a fitting place to lay the map out, wouldn't you say?" Bella asked nobody in particular; which was exactly who answered.

Just a few more steps until they reached the spot that only moments earlier had looked much wider and more welcoming. As they stepped into it, they all began mumbling about how the maze had deceived them again. Not only was this spot no wider, it didn't offer any other choice on which way to go as it had earlier seemed. Whether the Labyrinth had reshaped its layout before they reached the spot or their eyes were deceived, they could not tell. Whatever the reason, it was not what they had thought one turn earlier.

"Good grief!" Miriam groaned. Her constant comments were making everyone else unbearably annoyed.

"Let's eat first and then we'll check the maps," Pierce suggested.

Apparently, Bella had thought the same thing, for as the words left Pierce's mouth, Bella had already begun pulling things from under her cloak.

"Judah and Sam, I put some lunch things in both your bags. Could you pull them out? J, you have the Roota juice."

Sure enough, both the boys pulled bags from their cloaks, opened them up, and began pulling out all sorts of edible things.

"I'm amazed at how the cloaks carry these things," Judah commented, holding up a container of what looked to be granola squares. He peeled back the lid and held the bowl out for the others to take some of the odd-looking concoction.

Nobody wasted even a flit of a second but dipped straightaway into the plastic container, helping themselves to large chunks of the granola—or what looked like granola. As they filled their mouths with the unidentified mixture, delightful sounds started to be heard.

"Mmmm," and "this is good—what is this?" began to float around in the air.

"It's good, right?" Bella laughed as she stuffed more of the sweet concoction into her mouth, not noticing or caring as crumbs tumbled to the ground.

Again, the only one noticeably silent was Miriam. Not only was she silent as she ate, but she had also disappeared even further into her hood, which seemed odd. Perhaps she was pouting and felt like she could somehow hide from the others if she tucked herself away inside the dark, oversized hood.

Nobody was about to comment or suggest she pull it down. The truth was that everyone remained put off with her being there, and each was pleased that she'd decided to act like she wasn't there at all.

It would not be long before the rest of the Travelers had wished they too, had been tucked away in their cloak hoods, but for now, they were loud when they should have remained quiet, rambunctious when they should have stayed still, and careless when they should have been cautious.

They would become aware soon enough.

After a short time had passed and the group had completely stuffed themselves with sandwiches, Roota juice, the granola mixture, and a few other things, Bella packed one empty container into another until each one was neatly put away into the largest plastic bucket.

While Bella tidied up, Pierce pulled out two maps. Since there was only room on the ground for one, he tucked the other back into his cloak and spread out the other. There was hardly enough room in the cramped little space for both the map and the Travelers, so everyone except Pierce, Bella, and of course Miriam, stepped back.

Instantly Pierce's voice rang out. "Oh no!"

Bella's cry quickly followed. "This is terrible."

Miriam said nothing but even without being able to see her expression or hear her thoughts, it was evident that she was both displeased with Pierce and Bella, yet at the same time satisfied that she appeared to be right.

"What's going on?" Sam burst out. He tried to edge closer to see for himself, but the small space made it impossible for him, or anyone else, to get close to the map. Judah put his hand on Sam's wild hair.

"Sam, no worries kiddo, I'm sure Pierce and Bella have everything under control."

"As a matter of fact," Pierce spoke up somewhat less in control than everyone had hoped, "there's a huge problem over which I have no control and certainly no way to hide from any of you."

"WHAT DO YOU MEAN, a huge problem?" Sam shrieked wildly.

Matt, who'd been quiet for most twists and turns of the confusing maze, spoke calmly and mussed up Sam's already out-of-control hair. "Don't jump to horrible conclusions, Sammy." Then he edged as close to Pierce as space would allow. "What's going on Pierce?" he asked calmly. Matt, it seemed, was always calm.

Pierce's bony finger pointed down to the map.

"See that mark?" he asked. "That's where we are now." He waited until Matt indicated that he saw where Pierce was pointing.

"OK," Matt said, as though it was no big deal … like it was the same as every other map on any other day in any other land.

"Well, do you see any maze? Anything at all?" Pierce's voice got higher and higher as he asked the questions.

"Ummm," Matt replied, still calm."Now that you point it out, it looks like we should be standing in an open field."

"Yup," Pierce said with a shaky voice. "If this maze were part of the land, the map would have had the rocks and trees rise, and we would have seen it this morning. The map would have drawn a path for us through the maze." He looked at Bella, who was already looking at him. "The map showed no maze this morning, and it certainly shows no maze now."

"Mhm," Miriam finally mumbled. "Is the map showing us wrong? Maybe that's not where we are—that space on the map where you think it's us. What if that's not us?" Her tone changed slightly, but not enough to cause anyone to think she was genuinely trying to help but rather, to point out the grave error.

"Oh, that's where we are, all right," Bella said nervously, her voice shaking. "This maze is not a maze that Trilleah formed."

"What do you mean, 'Trilleah formed?'" Matt asked.

Jennifer couldn't tell if Matt was confused or if he was asking questions so the rest of the uninformed Travelers could understand what was happening without everyone asking questions all at once. Matt was brilliantly thoughtful like that.

Jennifer wondered for a minute if she should panic. While half the group seemed calm, the other half seemed about ready to come out of their skin. She chose a happy medium and allowed herself to become slightly worried, leaving plenty of room in case she needed to jump into a complete panic at a later time.

"What I'm saying is," Pierce replied to Matt, "this isn't a simple maze that we are just passing through." He took a big breath and continued trying to explain this unexplainable thing that even he didn't understand … yet.

Perfidiousness

"This is a Labyrinth!" Pierce squawked. "It's an intricate and twisted trap set specifically for catching something … or someone." The shallow explanation was not helping ease anyone's fears, so Bella jumped in but found she had nothing to add that would bring any amount of peace or calm back to the group—or to herself. She ended up mumbling a bunch of meaningless jargon but felt she had to try nevertheless.

"A Labyrinth is a carefully woven maze with only one way to the center." Bella had bent down and was trying to draw in the dirt to help her explanation make sense. "In a Labyrinth, the exit is not on the other side the way it would be in a maze." She sighed a loud, slow sigh, and stood up. "There's only one path and it is so complicated that if we reach the center, it's unlikely we can get back out. A Labyrinth is a heavily entwined and elaborate trap made up of lies and deceit."

Bella realized as the words slipped out that the more she tried to explain about a Labyrinth, the more fear she was stirring up, which was the exact opposite of what she'd wanted to do. She decided to abandon her explanation altogether and change the course of the conversation.

"Pierce, pull out the other map," she said. Bella picked up the one already spread out on the ground and tried to fold it, but the map refused to be folded; they'd seen this before. When the map had something the Travelers had not seen but which they needed to notice, the map would refuse to be folded. She put it back on the ground; there was no point in trying to fight it. If the map was not ready to be folded, it would not be folded. It would demand to be read and until they noticed whatever it was that it was trying to show, the fight would continue, wasting valuable time.

"What if we don't reach the center?" Sam whispered.

All eyes curiously turned from the map to Sam.

"Randomly stupid thought," Miriam snapped.

"Pardon?" Judah asked, as confused by the question as everyone else.

"Bella said if we reach the center we might not get back out, so what if we don't reach the center? What if we turn around now or find a new path?" Heads started nodding as each one made the connection and realized that Sam's question wasn't random after all, but instead, he was making some reasonable sense.

"Good question, Sam," Matt said, sounding pleased and rustling up Sam's crazy hair … again.

Heads began turning this way and straining to see that way, each looking for any sign of an exit or another way to go, but each finding the same thing—no other path than the one in front of them.

Pierce was not so excited about the question and gave a quick and disheartening answer. "I'm not sure it makes much difference if we get to the center of the Labyrinth or not. The point is, once inside, it's difficult—maybe even impossible—to get out." Again, Bella added more of an explanation because well, honestly, Pierce's explanation was quite disheartening.

"It's the intricacy and detail of the Labyrinth that makes it so hard to maneuver." As she was explaining, she happened to look past Sam and noticed something she decided not to point out at this particular time. What Bella didn't see was the path they had walked just a few moments earlier; it was gone. The tall, thick clusters of trees had moved, closing off that path and opening up another.

Oh, Shura. I could use your wisdom and understanding of this Labyrinth right now. Some insight into why we are in the midst of it and some answers about how we get out would be appreciated.

Her thoughts to Shura were interrupted by a shriek followed by gasps and squeals of both delight and terror. She turned away from Sam and toward the sounds. It seemed the Travelers had found what the map was trying to show; it also seemed that what they'd seen was outrageously horrifying and utterly delightful, both mixed up into one giant ball of confusion.

"It seems," Judah whispered, "that we are not the first to be caught in the perfidy of this Labyrinth." Jennifer piped in as well, having been quiet until now.

"There are others who are here or at least, it looks like there are other Travelers; but how can that be? Bella, have you ever seen others in Trilleah?" All eyes followed the words as they left Jennifer's mouth and traveled to Bella's ears. Everyone waited for an answer from the only one who might have one.

"Yes."

The answer couldn't be so simple, yet it was that simple. In fact, Bella had seen other Travelers on two occasions. Once she and Pierce came upon them, and they traveled together for a time but soon realized they were going in different directions. A second time she'd seen Travelers but only from a distance.

None of them had any awareness that there were plenty of Travelers who'd come before them; all who had failed to break the curse, losing their own lives instead.

"Yes?" Jennifer echoed the answer, apparently dissatisfied, and waited for more information.

"When you first came and I was showing you the rock covering the hollow, I mentioned that there were other hollows that we were unaware of; other hollows for other Travelers. You maybe don't remember your first time to Trilleah."

"I *do* remember, and I even remember you telling me about other hollows. I never thought much about it, I guess."

Bella moved closer to the map. "How do you know what you're seeing are Travelers, and how do you know they are in the center of the Labyrinth since it's not even on the map?" As the words rolled off of Bella's tongue, her eyes gazed down at the map and in an instant, she knew the answers to her own questions.

Clearly, on the map, tiny green lights were fading in and out. There were seven on the map right where they were standing, but a small way beyond that, there were six more blinking lights. They were so small and faded it was hard to see them at first, but once her eyes noticed them it was impossible not to see them. They became the focal point of the entire map.

"Well isn't that just great!" Miriam blurted out, still tucked into her hood. "We need to turn and head back out of this prison. It's closing in on us as we stand here and do nothing. We need to quit staring at a stupid map and get out of here." Miriam, usually bubbling over with anger and resentment, was finally showing a different emotion.

Sure, it came out sounding like anger but this time it was covered over with that one feeling so difficult to hide and impossible to ignore—fear.

Of course, the others assumed she was fearful of the Labyrinth. They assumed wrong, however, for what Miriam was frightened of was that perhaps some of these new Travelers just around the bend might have more knowledge of things in Trilleah; such things as Mindbenders and Reptilians and Shape-shifters, for example.

Miriam was horribly afraid that one of these new Travelers might recognize her and reveal the secrets she was working so hard to keep hidden.

Bella began shaking her head, recalling what she had seen behind them, thinking through her thoughts and choosing her words carefully. "We cannot turn back because … because … well, because the path we came in on is no longer there." Before the last sound rolled off of her tongue, every eye left the map and turned promptly to look behind her, where her own eyes had seen the horrifying truth.

Jennifer fought the tears that were demanding to be released, and her voice squeaked out the thought everyone else was thinking. "What are we going to do?"

Without thinking about his words at all, Judah answered. "We need to hush and find our Shailmas. We must hear them and follow their words. They always know what to do; they see from somewhere other than from where we see."

"I was just asking Shura for help," Bella replied, a bit of an excitement trickling from her voice. "You're right, Judah, the Shailmas are in the air; surely they see this Labyrinth from somewhere above and they must be able to see not only what's ahead but also the way out of this perfidious prison." The more she spoke, the more hope filled her.

"What about the others on the map?" Matt asked. "We can't just leave them. The maps show us only matters of importance; those things that are necessary for us to see."

"Matt's right," Judah said. "They are the reason the map refused to be folded. We can't ignore what the map showed us. It wouldn't be wise."

"Our Shailmas will know about them as well. We must search our souls and let our ears tune into the voices of the Shailmas. Only they will have the answers to such questions," Bella instructed. "We can't see ahead nor can we trust what is behind— but we can trust the Shailmas. They see what we cannot see and hear what we cannot hear. They know things too big for our minds to understand, and when we look for them they are always found, even if they do take too long most days."

Bella was ranting on and on about the Shailmas. What, at first seemed like an effort to bring hope to the Travelers, soon began to appear more like she was trying to comfort her own raging soul.

One by one each Traveler disappeared back into the loneliness of their hoods. Each wondered the same thing. Should they have stayed hidden this whole time? Was Miriam aware of something they were not? Perhaps she wasn't pouting, after all. Perhaps she knew of some danger lurking ahead that they did not know of … until now.

Blind Obedience

After many awkward moments, Miriam spoke up. She hoped that by seeming eager to meet the new Travelers, she could use it to her advantage later. Even if someone did recognize her, she decided this was her best chance to avoid suspicion.

"We need to find the other Travelers."

Every head turned toward her, knowing she was right but perturbed she was the one who had said it. Jennifer wanted to respond. She wanted to scream at Miriam and tell her she had no business suggesting such a thing or even accuse her of being part of setting up this whole trap. Instead, she stayed quiet and pleaded with Simeon to give her answers—or at least direction.

Simeon, you can see this whole Labyrinth, both the way in and the way out, and I know there IS a way out. There has to be a way out. We need to know which way to go, who's up ahead, and if we go to them or stay away. Jennifer listened harder than she'd ever listened before.

Simeon's earlier words echoed back to her now. *It is not I who is silent, Little One, but rather you who doesn't listen.*

"But what if they're not friendly?" Sam reasoned. "What if they're not who we think they are? What if they're part of the trap?"

"What if they're the bait in the Labyrinth?"

They all heard the words and looked around to see who had said them; the voice wasn't as familiar as it should have been. Nobody seemed to have said the words, yet it was odd that they'd all heard them. Certainly, somebody had spoken them, but nobody wanted to claim them. How odd; how very, very odd.

Jennifer tried tuning out the worries of her companions; she tried calming her fears; she listened hard for the voice of her Shailma.

"Simeon, help," she whispered over and over again.

"The map showed us for a reason," Judah said, trying hard to comfort Sam and the others. He was not comforted himself, so he doubted anyone else was either. Their confidence in the maps was shaken considerably, so trying to find comfort in it regarding these other Travelers seemed an unreasonable task.

After a few words from this one or some far-fetched explanation from that one—all trying to make sense of such nonsense—Jennifer spoke up.

"I agree with Miriam." Even as she forced the words out of her mouth, she felt all eyes jerk toward her, either surprised that she'd spoken up, or confused that she would agree with Miriam. Either way, it didn't matter. Jennifer had heard from Simeon, so even if she had to go alone, she would go.

Little One, Simeon whispered in her mind, *Miriam is right. The map has shown you for a reason, a reason you will know soon enough. For now, it is you who must lead these frightened ones; they will not follow Miriam, and they don't have the courage to go themselves. You must lead them.*

Jennifer questioned her Shailma's instruction, knowing it was a useless discussion. She was either going to follow the directions of the only one she trusted, or she wasn't. The direction had been given; it was up to her whether to follow it or not. Jennifer decided that if she trusted Simeon, and indeed she did, she had to follow his lead and do what he was asking.

OK Simeon, but only if you go with me and promise that you will not be silent.

I will lead you, Little One. Jennifer grinned an enormous grin, not because of the words he spoke in the secret place of her soul, but because he did speak. Simeon was indeed with her.

"We must go now," Jennifer said loudly to the others whom she could still feel staring at her. She did not wait for arguments or questions but instead felt tugged at by Simeon to get moving.

All I need to do is move my feet; Simeon will do the rest. He will lead, I will follow, no turning back. The more she repeated this in her mind, the more she believed it. The more she believed it, the more confident she became, not in herself, but in her Shailma. Certainly, Simeon would not leave her nor lead her astray.

"Let's go," she urged as she edged past the Travelers.

Jennifer took many steps in what appeared to be the wrong direction, although any direction seemed like the wrong one at this point. She turned around, only half-expecting anyone to be following her. She was only half-disappointed when she saw that no one was. She hesitated, as if wanting to say something, but then feeling Simeon tug at her to keep going, Jennifer turned and began walking again. Her feet were stumbling and she was grateful for the cloak that hid her trembling knees and missteps.

Even through the thickness of her hood, she heard Judah's voice while he stood back with the others, watching as she walked ahead. "I may not be sure about this direction, but I am sure about my sister. I'm following her." Jennifer's legs steadied a bit, and a smile pulled at the edges of her mouth. She let out a small sigh, not realizing until the breath had escaped that she'd been holding it in.

Within only a few steps, Jennifer felt Judah beside her. If she could count on no one else, she could count on Judah.

"Jelly Bean," he whispered. Just hearing him comforted her soul. "I don't doubt you; I'm curious, though, what made you head this direction?"

"Simeon is leading me," she said calmly. "It's like I can see him but not with my eyes as I see you." She tried to explain, knowing she wouldn't be able to. Then, an interesting comment tumbled from her lips, one that Judah took seriously and would ponder time and time again while they remained caught in the Labyrinth. "I'm not leading anyone Judah; I'm following the one who is leading me and hoping the rest of you will come as well."

The statement gave Judah a glimpse of just how close Jennifer had become to Simeon. He wondered if her unique ability to trust her Shailma and follow him, seemingly at any cost, was the reason they needed her to be in Trilleah. He didn't know why—none of them did—but for whatever reason, it was essential she was here.

While they walked in outer silence, their inner thoughts twisted and turned. While Jennifer was intent on keeping her sights on Simeon, Judah was remembering back to the conversation he'd had with Bella about bringing Jennifer to Trilleah in the first place.

When Bella first brought up Jennifer's inclusion in their strange travels, Judah had refused. "Absolutely not!" He would not even consider it. But Bella had continued to push him about bringing her to Trilleah, and Judah knew in his belly that she was right. For reasons not yet revealed to any of them, Jennifer's presence in Trilleah was altogether necessary to free the cursed souls of the Waiting Ones.

She was so young but then again, so was he. Jennifer was so childish and gullible and naive … she'd believe nearly anything and anybody. She had a simple trust and deep imagination that made both Judah and their auntie curious. Perhaps these were all reasons for her to be in Trilleah. But now in what Judah had just seen—such boldness, such leadership, such trust in Shailmas—these seemed necessary qualities for the leader that she was most certainly becoming.

With her brother beside her, Jennifer heard shuffling behind her and knew without turning to look that the others had decided to come along. "Thanks, Simeon," she whispered inside her hood. Her ears never heard any response, but the eyes of her heart watched a smile cross Simeon's face and she felt his pleasure fill her cloak. That was enough for her. Her Shailma was leading her and Jennifer was more than grateful. She was determined to follow him, no matter where he may lead.

Jennifer suddenly felt crowded. She knew the others had chosen to follow her, but did they have to stay so close? Her heels kept getting stepped on by whoever was right behind her. She wanted to turn and tell the Travelers to back up, but she didn't. The truth was that she was so glad they had decided to follow her she didn't mind the odd kick to the back of her boot. It gave Jennifer confidence knowing she wasn't alone.

The path was narrow in the Labyrinth, but the deeper into the center they wandered, the more narrow and dark it became. Before long, the space was only wide enough for one Traveler at a time, so Judah fell back and tucked himself in closely behind his sister.

It became so dark that Jennifer had to slow down and keep her hands out in front of her, feeling for bits of tree or brush that may be sticking out. More than once she tripped; more than once the line of Travelers following banged into her as she'd slow down or dart around a branch or other debris.

Jennifer wanted to turn around and share her growing fears with the others but was afraid that if she attempted to turn around, the others might trample right over her. She swallowed her fears and kept walking—taking this corner and that one, right, left, turn, left, right, turn.

Kaija Mae

"Simeon," Jennifer whispered; she meant for no one to hear but her Shailma. "This is getting too hard. I want to be bold and fearless … I really do. But I'm neither bold nor fearless." She paused. "In fact, I'm weak and terrified."

I'm still here, Little One.

Why can't I see you? Jennifer asked, only a little bit relieved that he had responded. *I need to see you.* She was hoping for more.

Do you believe you can see me? Simeon asked. *Don't try harder, for it's not in the trying, Little One.* This confused Jennifer, and without her saying any words, Simeon saw her confusion and continued explaining the unexplained.

Jenny, in the land of Trilleah, it's not trying harder that makes anything happen—or not happen. It's not in hoping deeper or working harder. It's in believing that you hear, see, feel, succeed, gain victories. You ask the wrong questions, Little One. Ask instead for me to help you believe.

You cannot make yourself believe; you must ask to believe. Ask me to help you believe, Little One. The more you hear me, the deeper your belief grows; like the roots of a tree going deeper and deeper. Remember when you first arrived at Trilleah? Remember, Jenny, how you did not even know what the eyes of your heart were?

Simeon's voice was becoming louder even while it remained only in her mind. It was more reassuring and suddenly the eyes of her heart were opened, and she could see him again. *Yes, I do remember!* She let out a giggle at remembering that first trip to the strange land. Oh, how much she'd changed since then.

You learned to hear me a little bit at a time. It was not that I wasn't speaking—I talked to you often. You did not yet believe, even a shred. She wasn't sure, but Jennifer thought she heard a laugh come from Simeon.

All of this silent conversation between Jennifer and her Shailma kept her from noticing the light that was beginning to poke back onto the path. But when her eyes thought they caught a glimpse of the other Travelers—the ones they saw on the map—she stopped suddenly. Judah ran into the back of her so hard that she tumbled to the ground. Jennifer mumbled. It took her a moment, but soon she got her footing back and straightened herself up.

Now with only a small ray of light poking its head through the overgrown brush above them, Jennifer turned around. She no longer wanted to be at the front of this little parade but saw no way of changing that.

"Look … Up there!" She pointed her hand out in front of her, trying to catch enough light so the group could see where "up there," actually was.

"Up where?" Sam asked. Jennifer couldn't see what was going on behind her but if she could have, she would have noticed everyone straining their necks to see past her and all that was in front of them, blocking their view almost entirely.

It seemed to Jennifer that Sam's voice should have contained some fear or nervousness. Instead, she thought it was an excitement that dressed his words. She could hear much chatter behind her now, and she felt her own feet speed up a noticeable amount. "Up there" was becoming closer and closer. The group of what looked like new Travelers a few moments earlier now evolved into faces.

It was beginning to feel like they were walking into the den of a thousand lions. With each step, the Travelers were going deeper into the Labyrinth and honestly, none of them knew for certain if there was a way out. It seemed like it was a living, breathing perfidy. Lies and deceit were spreading in every direction, like the fine threads of a spider web laid out precisely, the prey becoming more ensnared with each step.

"Does it feel like this Labyrinth is alive?" Sam asked.

"It does, Sam, now that you put it that way," Matt answered. "It seems like the walls have eyes and are watching us," he added. "I can nearly feel its breath on the back of my neck."

It did seem like the Labyrinth had a watchful eye. "I think it's the new Travelers up ahead that have the watchful eyes," Bella whispered. "Look!"

Their eyes all focused straight ahead—now only a few feet to where this group stood—and indeed, every eye had spotted them and seemed to be staring straight through them.

"Creepy," Pierce mumbled. "Why are they staring like that?"

Jennifer wished she wasn't the one at the front of this parade and wanted to close her eyes so tight that she disappeared. She knew, however, if she closed her eyes at all, she would tumble over the thick brush covering the ground, and sprawl right into the center of the gawking group of strangers.

They looked harmless … quite ordinary, in fact … pretty much the same as the Travelers who were following close behind her. But in this land, one could never be sure about anything or anyone. Miriam had been with them for quite some time now, and they were still unsure of her. How would they ever know if these new Travelers could be trusted?

Jennifer felt something pushing at her from the side; she began to feel annoyed and impatient. When she turned and saw it was Bella and Pierce trying to squeeze past her, she moved over as far as she could. She gladly let them both scoot by. Jennifer was so thankful to be rescued from this uncomfortable meeting that she couldn't think of even one nasty thing to say to Pierce.

"Thank you," was all she muttered as they stepped in front of her. He gave no reply. Instead, he spoke to the strangers now upon them.

"How long have you been here?" Pierce asked the one who seemed to be the leader of the new, wide-eyed group.

"We've been stuck here, right in this very spot, for nearly three hours," came the sweetest voice ever. "My name is Kaija Mae," and she thrust her hand toward Bella and Pierce. Bella reached out and shook it.

Jennifer sensed an instant connection with Kaija Mae for an odd reason she couldn't explain, at least not yet, but the connection was undeniable. It felt like the two had been the very best of friends in some other life before this one; altogether unexplainable.

"I have many family members trapped in Malleana Forest, and we can't even help because we are stuck in this stupid maze."

Kaija Mae chattered on and on; rambling foolish jibberish. "Do you know the way out? How did you know we were here?"

Jennifer laughed to herself. In less than one minute of coming upon Kaija Mae, Jennifer realized why she had been so annoying to the Travelers her first time to Trilleah. Kaija Mae reminded Jennifer of her earlier self with the unending list of questions and the habit of not waiting for answers to one before asking the next.

Sam's elbow swiftly but playfully found Jennifer's ribs. "She reminds me of you," he said with a serious voice.

"Oh Sam, that's ridiculous," she replied, not about to admit that he was right.

There was a lengthy exchange of words between Pierce, Bella, and Kaija Mae. Jennifer found most of it boring and tuned it out. Instead, she spun around and began asking Matt her own list of unimportant questions. Matt was as kind as always. However, it was apparent that, unlike her, he was not ignoring the conversation going on up ahead. Even though he answered Jennifer's endless questions, his attention was certainly not on her.

She felt disheartened and eventually let her questions with Matt end, and instead turned to Sam to continue her barrage of chatter. It had dawned on her recently, during the long quiet trudging through the Labyrinth, that she didn't know any of the Travelers very well; she determined in her mind to change that and this seemed like the opportunity to do just that.

Sam, unlike Matt, was not paying any attention to the conversation between the two groups of Travelers and was freely participating in the meaningless jibber-jabber with Jennifer.

She fidgeted with this and that, rolling a piece of something or other that she'd found inside of her cloak between her fingers until she'd made a little ball. Jennifer was very content being non-existent in her surroundings. Very content that is, until a most unusual thing called for her attention. A sound. It entered her ears, small and barely noticeable at first, but quickly became louder and louder until she could no longer ignore it.

What is that? she wondered. It was a sound, but it seemed that Jennifer could see it as well; not with her eyes so much, as seeing something outside of herself such as a bee or a tree rustling its leaves, and not with the eyes of her heart, but then again, it must have been. Regardless, the noise that had come to her ears was also visible to her soul.

Jennifer's attention was at full throttle now as she focused on figuring out what exactly this was. She could hear Sam in the background continue to ramble, but she paid him no mind.

A mist, I suppose, she heard her thoughts suggest, yet she did not remember thinking it. *A mist,* she thought again. Indeed, it was her own thought this time. *What kind of mist? Why are you in my ear? How can I see you if you are a sound?* How inconveniently confusing. Dreadful. Purely dreadful.

As the thought lingered and danced and twisted into a bit of a knot, her mind demanded an answer. Knowing she couldn't force an answer to a question such as this one, another thought followed the first … more of an idea, really.

Perhaps this is not a sound that I can see but rather a sight that I can hear. Indeed, this idea was the truth. As she pondered which inconceivable thing it was—a sound she could see or a sight she could hear—the spectacle became bigger and bolder. Furthermore, she noticed a being, bright and distinct, standing between the two groups of Travelers; a light almost, but clearly in the shape of a mortal.

For a few seconds, this bright misty figure stood as if to keep the two groups separated. Nobody else seemed to see it, and while Jennifer kept her eyes fastened to it, she could hear Sam continue to chatter on to her, even though she was no longer listening. Bella and Pierce continued talking with Kaija Mae.

So far, Kaija Mae was the only person from the group of new Travelers who'd spoken at all.

Most likely because she gives no one else a chance to say anything, Jennifer thought.

She could hear whispering from behind but dared not turn around. She did, however, push her hood back slightly and turn her head enough to let Judah know she had something to say. Not once did her eyes wander from this radiant being who continued to stand silently in the gap.

"Uh, Judah," she whispered, for truly she wanted no other ears to hear. "Do you see something unusual in front of Pierce and Bella?" She waited impatiently for Judah's response.

She heard nothing.

Slowly turning her head a little more but still not enough to let her eyes lose sight of this illuminated essence that now appeared to be staring right at her, she repeated her question—a bit louder this time. She dared not flinch nor let anyone else hear her question … especially the one who had Jennifer in its sights.

Because You Believe

"Jelly Bean," he whispered, "are you talking about the other Travelers? Of course, I can see them," Judah said. Even though Jennifer couldn't see Judah's face, she was sure that he was rolling his eyes or making some ridiculous facial expression, thinking her a bit of a loon.

Unswayed, she took a step back and continued her hushed conversation with her brother. Jennifer's eyes were beginning to ache, but she was determined to keep them on this being that had come to her awareness.

"No, not Kaija Mae. In front of her; between them and us," she explained.

"No," Judah answered her. "There is nothing between them and us."

"OK," was all she bothered to reply. She wasn't sure if she should feel privileged that she was the only one who seemed to see such a sight or upset by the same thought. *It's not a dark and shadowy thing*, she reasoned to herself. *I think it must be a good something; it must be.*

As she continued her back-and-forth reasoning, mostly to make herself feel brave—which was not working nearly as well as she'd hoped—a sound came to her mind once more.

You do see me, Little One. Don't be afraid. I am not from Trilleah. I've been sent from the Great Light to bring you out of this perfidious Labyrinth.

It was not distinct words which she heard, such as when she heard Simeon; her ears were not involved whatsoever. It was more like a thought that had somehow been inserted into whatever place it was that thoughts came from, yet she knew it was not a thought; not her own, anyway. It was more like a bubble of thought that someone had blown in. It was almost as if she knew what the unrecognized being was thinking. Yes, that was it; she knew the thought of the one thinking it.

Jennifer turned to tell Judah about it but then stopped and turned back. She knew there would be no way to describe either the lighted presence or how she had known its thoughts—no way at all. She sighed, frustrated at all these things she could not explain. As she thought about how many things she could not tell anyone, Jennifer began to feel very alone.

The chatter continued between Kaija Mae and Bella as if they were old friends. As Jennifer listened, she wondered why she could see this being when no one else could. As she pondered the wondering, the answer fell into her mind; again as though she knew the thoughts of this lighted being.

Because you believe, Little One.

Suddenly, the question of believing became of utmost importance and Jennifer's mind began to spin with a wonderment of belief.

Is my imagination so great, she wondered of herself, *that I could make things appear just by believing they exist? I don't understand.* She could feel herself getting overwhelmed and Jennifer decided right then and there to quit trying to figure out those things that had no answers. It seemed difficult at first, but the longer she pondered her new ideas, the more simple it became; the more satisfied her mind was and the more rest she felt.

Jennifer inhaled deeply, refreshing her lungs and stilling her mind. It felt so wonderful that she breathed in another and let it escape slowly through her nostrils. It felt as though she were inhaling peace and exhaling anxiousness. Jennifer went through this cycle a few more times but on about the fifth inhaling, and only for a very brief second, she felt a warm wind encircle her and touch her eyes.

She felt it; like gentle fingers wiped across her eyelids. There was no doubt about it. Something had come in that warm breeze and touched her eyes. Jennifer knew this for sure because, at precisely the same moment, she saw many things that she was sure nobody else saw. If anyone else had seen what her eyes now noticed, they'd have said so. Nobody did.

Jennifer knew she'd been given a brief glimpse, for some reason, into what was surrounding them; a glimpse into some other world that now joined with her own. She had heard that one who touched her eyes, speak, and what it said both baffled and intrigued her.

"I've opened the eyes of your heart so that you will become enlightened to the path that is before you," were the words her heart had heard. What they meant, she was not sure yet.

Jennifer began seeing small black shadows everywhere. There were far too many to count, but each was distinct and looked similar to a stingray. They had faces, horrible faces, with nasty, long yellow teeth covered in slime. The teeth were gnashing out at the Travelers. They looked as though they were trying to get to the Travelers but could not quite reach them.

These things were so hideous that Jennifer knew she didn't imagine them for never, even in her most horrible imaginings, would she be able to come up with such grotesque and horrible beings. The sights her eyes were seeing came and went so quickly that she did not have time to panic. Like flashes of lightning—there one minute and gone the next.

She looked directly ahead at the glowing presence still hovering between Pierce and Bella, and Kaija Mae, and knew it was this one that had touched her eyes, opening them to see the unseen. She could not pick out features in the being, particularly, like a nose or ears. However, she did sense a pair of eyes looking out from the light and directly into her soul. She was captivated by whatever this was and the more she looked, the more peace she felt pour over her.

Jennifer couldn't make herself look away.

She didn't want to.

As she stared, trying to look deeper into the glow, she saw something come from out of its center. Like a giant bubble being blown, a shield grew bigger and bigger until it entirely surrounded the Travelers. It started at Bella and Pierce, and then as though it was being pulled back to cover them all, Jennifer watched as it went directly overtop of her. She turned and made her eyes follow it past Judah, past Matt and Sam, and finally past Miriam.

It surrounded them on all sides, and she knew—from the glow—that none of the slimy creatures she'd glimpsed in those lightning flashes would be able to reach them. A second bubbling shield came from the glowing presence and went the other direction, covering Kaija Mae and those that stood behind her.

The bright glowing form faded into nothing more than the tiniest of dots, and then with one quick flash, it was gone. Also gone was the shield she'd just seen cover the Travelers.

Only gone from your sight, Jennifer heard Simeon whisper to her. *It will be back in your view soon enough.* When she heard his quiet voice, she became angry.

Why did you let us come here? she demanded. *Why can't you and the other Shailmas lead us out?* Jennifer's eyes instantly stung and threatened to unlatch the gate that would release ten thousand tears—something she did not wish to have happen. At least, with these new Travelers—and Matt—standing close enough to see such a pathetic and embarrassing display of weakness.

She blinked hard and then thankfully, became distracted by the commotion that was rising around her. As Kaija Mae and some of her Travelers continued talking with Bella and Pierce, she again saw the black mists swarming above them.

From out of nowhere, these shadowy creatures crowded down upon the Travelers; all of the Travelers. It was evident that they were not targeting either group, but they swarmed everywhere and included everybody. They began to swoop down toward the groups and as they came closer, Jennifer noticed something peculiar.

Their eyes.

She had supposed they'd have black eyes or red eyes like other wretched creatures she'd seen in Trilleah but, in fact, they seemed to have no eyes at all—just deep, black holes that looked like they went right through. Jennifer could see right through them in the place where she'd assume they should have eyes.

If they are what the glowing presence touched my eyes to see, she reasoned even in the midst of her panic, *then the shield must be here as well.* She began squinting and very much wanted to stretch out her hands to see if she could touch it.

She was contemplating doing so in her mind when they all heard a loud *thud*. Then another. *Thud.* Another and another and another. It sounded like back home when they'd sit in the living room and suddenly hear a big raven crash into the window.

As the Travelers shifted their eyes toward the sound, they saw what was making such a racket.

No one knew what was going on, at least as far as Jennifer could tell, although she quickly decided that if her Shailma had shown her, it was entirely possible the other Shailmas had shown their Travelers as well. However, from the expressions that began smearing across their half-hidden faces, it seemed she was the only one who'd seen the truth of what was around them.

The *thuds* they heard time and time and time again were loud. Each one echoed, making it just that much louder under the clear dome.

Matt shouted, covering his ears. "What's happening?" Many voices responded at once with similar answers.

"I don't know," one said.

"Who knows?" shrieked another.

Jennifer said nothing, but in her mind she was thinking quick answers to each anxious word. *I know*, was her thought, but how does one describe what her eyes had seen? *They'd all think I had gone mad,* she reasoned with herself before deciding to keep quiet.

Maybe she had gone mad after all.

Seeing in Spirit

twenty eight

Judah moved beside her and put his hand on her arm.

"Jelly Bean," he said loudly. "Are you OK?" Jennifer had been so busy wondering whether to share what she'd seen or not, that she was oblivious to everyone's conversations about her and hadn't heard any of their questions.

Well, she supposed the question she'd been wondering about had been decided for her. She took a deep breath and opened her mouth, hoping she'd be able to explain without looking crazy.

"I saw them before they started darting at us," were the words that came from her mouth. Jennifer knew as she heard them, that the words make no sense.

"Saw what, dear?" Kaija Mae asked so sweetly. "Tell us what you saw, darling … what are you talking about?" Poor thing. She truly did remind Jennifer of herself.

"Just before …" she began explaining. "When you were talking with Bella, something touched my eyes and I was able to see all these black withery beings hanging in the air. They weren't darting at us then, mostly just hovering about. They have no eyes so I don't know how they see us—maybe they don't."

"What has no eyes, Jennifer?" Pierce demanded. She tried to explain what it was that she'd seen earlier, but the Travelers were getting annoyed, as her explanations were far more confusing than informative.

"Maybe that's why they're bumping into each other," Sam said, his voice still shaky. Perhaps he did understand what she was trying to explain—at least a little.

They're not running into each other, Sam," Jennifer said. "I also saw a bright light standing just between you, Auntie Bella, and Kaija Mae. It told me—sort of— that it was here to lead us out of the Labyrinth and then it blew an enormous shield around us.

That's what they are running into, Sam. That's what's making the banging sounds."

Even as the words were coming from Jennifer's mouth, she knew it sounded absurd and doubted anyone would believe her. Except … the flying creatures were there, now equally visible to everyone. They wanted an explanation, and they got one. However crazy it may have sounded, no one else offered one, which left Jennifer's description as the most reasonable one available.

The Travelers were still worked up and panicked, but a little less than before Jennifer mentioned the shield. It would be supposed that any idea of a shield to block the enemy would be a calming thought, although certainly not the answer to their dilemma. If they could have all seen it, of course, it would have eliminated their fear altogether. But like most things in Trilleah, the Travelers had to believe without seeing.

After a moment of pondering, Sam spoke again. "Did this glowing thing tell you how to get out of here?" As the words shot out of his mouth, his voice got higher and higher until it was barely more than a squeak.

"No, it did not," Jennifer mumbled. Sighs and cries bounced off of the invisible shield and became thunderous inside the bubble.

Even as she answered Sam, and saw his face cover over with disappointment, Jennifer had a knowing in her belly that they'd get out, and also that they were very close to a clay tablet. She didn't understand how she knew either of these things since the thoughts never came to her as one would expect a thought to come —nobody said anything of the sort—she just knew; not in her mind, not in her heart, but somewhere else altogether. In another part of her that she didn't know existed, she had a knowing.

You know it in your spirit, Little One, she heard Simeon say loud and clear.

In my what? Jennifer questioned.

Your spirit, she heard again. Simeon must have noticed her confusion and immediately started in with an explanation. *You, like everyone else, have a body,* Simeon began. *People, in their limited knowledge, take great care of their body. They feed it and spend money and time making the body look appealing. They often make it their god. You all mistakingly believe that your bodies are all there is to you.* Simeon chuckled—which Shailmas rarely do—but Jennifer knew he had.

What are you talking about, Simeon? Jennifer pondered deeply, since he'd spun her mind into a web of confusion by now. All she wanted to do was get out of this Labyrinth and get back to the hollow. Surely all this explaining could wait for another time.

This thing I'm telling you about, your body, is merely a shell of what is important, Jenny, of who you really are. Deep inside of every mortal is something much more important. It is your spirit.

It is with your spirit that you hear me, and with it, you see all that you see here. It is with your spirit that you saw the light and it's with your spirit that you hear me now. You know that you see the things here in Trilleah with the eyes of your heart, and you know that your heart does not have eyes. Have you never wondered then, how you understand any of this?

She had not wondered, to be honest. But now that Simeon had gone off on a bit of a rant about it all, she'd become quite curious.

It's how you are going to get out of the Labyrinth. It is the place where you know what you know about the light and about what you saw and heard. It's in that place where you will find your way because that light, that spirit you saw, is with you, even though you don't see it now. It is the shield of protection that surrounds you and the others.

Jennifer was even more confused than before, but she knew that Simeon had never given her wrong information, and she also knew that everything he told her was for her good not for her downfall. She decided to trust him on this too.

"OK, Simeon," was all she muttered, but she was sincere, and Simeon knew it. Her *OK* meant truly, that it was, in fact, OK. It was acceptable to her whether she understood or not, and she would follow her spirit.

Sam's voice demanded her attention just then. She knew they had to get out of here before the Travelers began panicking and fighting against each another. What they needed now was to stick together, not fall apart and start quarreling.

"I've got to get out of here!" Sam screamed. Pierce's big, ugly hand shot out of his cloak and connected with Sam's shoulder.

"Ouch!" the boy wailed.

"Hush up," Pierce whispered, although, even in a whisper everyone could tell he was angry.

"Sam," Bella said, using her sweetest voice, "we're going to get out of here right now." She threw such a glare toward Pierce that he knew to keep his hands inside his cloak and his mouth shut.

Suddenly, Jennifer remembered the locket that was hanging around her neck; the one Matt had given her. With both hands she reached up and grabbed it, holding it tightly. It gave Jennifer a small measure of courage, thinking of her mamma and the very reason she was in Trilleah.

"This way," she said and began moving quickly down one of the openings.

"Was this opening here the whole time?" Matt asked. He moved close to Jennifer, and she was happy that he did. She looked into his face and remembered back to yesterday when he'd shown up at her birthday and kissed her. Even though it was only on the forehead, he had kissed her nonetheless, and a large smile spread across her face.

She let go of the locket and realized that he'd asked a question that she did not answer, so she answered now.

"I don't remember, Matt, but it's here now, and we are going to use it." Even though she said the words, she knew that it wasn't here before. It had somehow opened up to them and in what she now understood to be her spirit, she knew to follow it. What she did not know was if anyone would follow her. They always had in the past, and she was hoping they would again now.

After all, she reasoned with herself, *it was Pierce who brought them into the Labyrinth in the first place, not me.* Anything she could blame on him, she would.

"Jennifer," she heard someone say. She turned slightly.

"What?" she replied.

As soon as she realized the voice belonged to Miriam, she wished she had ignored it. Nothing good ever came from Miriam, after all.

Eyes that See

"Why are *you* deciding which way to go?" Miriam demanded.

Jennifer ignored her.

"I mean, why do *you* think you know the way out?"

Again, Jennifer ignored her; partly because it was Miriam, and partly because Jennifer didn't have any reasonable answers. She had no idea why she was the one leading them, but she did know that was the way it was supposed to be, at least for now.

"Simeon," she muttered inside her cloak. "Why *am* I the one leading the Travelers? I don't want to be here at all, not in the Labyrinth, not in Trilleah, not in this stupid cloak." Suddenly the reasons came to her as she heard Simeon's voice.

Jenny, it's because you believe.

"Huh?" she said loud enough for Judah to take notice. He looked at her but said nothing.

You believe that you hear me, you believe what your eyes see, and you believe what your ears hear. Then Jennifer's Shailma told her something she would remember for at least as long as the rest of this journey and probably even a bit longer than that.

The bright light of the Spirit appeared before everyone Jenny; every Traveler could have seen it if the eyes of their hearts would have been open to it and their hearts would have believed. You are the one who saw it because you believe that such things are possible and when the eyes of your heart are opened, those unseen things become seen.

But Simeon, she began to argue, *I didn't even know I had eyes of my heart until Bella and the others taught me of them. How is it then that I see what they are unable to?*

It's not that they are unable, Little One, he replied, although he seemed to be getting slightly impatient. *They are unwilling. There is a tremendous difference between the two. You would do well to remember that.*

Question after question tumbled in her mind—like clothes in a dryer—but Simeon gave no more answers to any of them. Instead, he gave one simple command—easy to follow, hard to argue with. *Jennifer, stop asking why and start moving your feet. You will know which way to go, but you must go. The way will not be revealed as long as you stand here and wait. It will only be revealed as you go.*

But Simeon, she continued in her usual pattern of arguing instead of obeying. Simeon made it even clearer.

Jennifer ... GO ...

That was clear enough. Even though Jennifer was not comfortable leading, and even though she grumbled and mumbled under her breath, she went. She knew Simeon well enough to understand when it was time to stop questioning and start obeying.

They were still going in the same direction as when they began walking a few moments ago. Jennifer hoped Kaija Mae and the new group of Travelers had followed, but she wasn't sure and didn't waste even a moment to turn and find out. Miriam, on the other hand, was very close behind her and continued to pester Jennifer about her being in the lead.

Jennifer wondered if she was angry about it—jealous perhaps—or if she genuinely wanted to know. Either way, Jennifer continued to ignore her; that is until Miriam moved closer and was right beside Jennifer. She turned her head to see that Miriam had also turned her head and was staring at her. As the girls' eyes met, a chill snaked its way through Jennifer's blood; she grew cold from the outside inward.

Miriam's eyes had lost their color and had become a dull gray. As she spoke, and Jennifer could not be entirely sure of what she was seeing, it looked as if Miriam was having difficulty keeping her tongue inside of her mouth. It looked like that tongue wanted to lash out and choke the life out of Jennifer. Miriam's gray eyes stared into Jennifer's own and somehow burrowed straight into her soul.

Jennifer was so focused on what she was seeing and struggling to make it clear in her mind, that she nearly missed the words being seethed out toward her. The only part she did hear was the very last bit.

"Do not think you'll be the leader for long, Miss Jennifer. Surely evil will overtake you and you will be no more."

"Huh?" Jennifer's ears were pierced with the words and she felt a sharp sting on her right cheek. If she were going to believe everything she saw, then she would have to believe that, quicker than a wink, a dull, yellow tongue had lashed out from Miriam's mouth and struck her on the cheek, feeling like a hot poker burning her flesh. Jennifer could not possibly believe such a thing, although as she brought one hand up to press against her stinging cheek, she felt a few drops of blood.

"Tell no one of this," were the foul words that spewed from Miriam and as she spoke them, she brought up one finger and touched Jennifer's lips. Jennifer instantly smelled sulfur and it felt like a hot coal had touched her mouth. She jerked her head back and tried to scream but no sound came out. She tried again, terrified and desperate to warn the others about Miriam, but she could not make herself speak; not even a word.

Jennifer turned, desperately searching for Judah. Seeing that he'd taken a place somewhere near the end of this single-file parade, she tried to stop and move back toward him, but the group would not have it. They kept walking, pushing her to keep going.

Something inside of her said, *turn left*, although as she looked left, there was no path. Her eyes were burning with hot tears that were rolling down her cheeks and she spoke angrily, although no sound came from her tongue. *There's no path to the left.*

Before all the words had been thought in her mind, and even though her vision was becoming blurred by the flow of stinging tears, Jennifer saw what she saw and nobody would ever convince her she hadn't.

A hand swooped down from the air—somewhere above the Labyrinth but inside of the shield—and pulled the wall of trees aside, just like it was a breezy little curtain. Then, right before her and directly to the left, a path was exposed. *This is crazy and unbelievable and scary and horrible and altogether marvelous*, she thought.

As she turned her head to find Judah, she saw instead that Miriam had taken a spot directly behind her, blocking her from the others. As their eyes met again, Jennifer noticed that the deep green had returned to Miriam's eyes and she smiled the sweetest smile. Jennifer would have thought she'd gone mad if it were not for the yellow-forked tongue that peeked out through Miriam's phony smile. Although it didn't fight to escape this time, it was there, nevertheless.

Jennifer turned back, her own eyes large with terror, but determined to follow the knowing in her spirit and get them out of this perfidious Labyrinth for no other reason than to get Judah and Bella—and the rest of the Travelers—to be aware that there was a devilish traitor among them. They would know what to do. Jennifer touched her cheek again and wiped the blood away with the sleeve of her cloak. Her lips continued to burn.

The Travelers were exhausted. They'd been caught in this trap far too long. To say they were concerned would be too light a word, for truly they were in deep anguish, at least some of them were. The others were downright terrified; not terrified of creatures or beings or evil kings, for indeed none of these things had made an appearance here in the confines of the Labyrinth.

Since they had become caught in this perfidy, the land had been quiet—too quiet. They'd seen no shrew rats, no vexaturs, no Trows, no farathins and no fliers. Furthermore, and to their great relief, they had not seen nor heard a thing from the king or his armies. Perhaps that was because it was the king himself who had set the trap and if they could calculate correctly, their time was quickly tick-tocking itself away. Surely, that was the whole intention of the king. After all, he didn't need to kill the Travelers or vaporize them as he'd done to Matt on the last visit. He didn't even need to scare them.

All King Shrailzhar had to do was keep them trapped by the perfidy of the Labyrinth long enough that the sun would set, and the gates of Solstice would close before they could get out. That was all that was required for the Travelers to be finished and the king's dark land to be safe forever.

It was just a few more hours before their souls would be added to the Forest of Malleana and there would be no Curse Breakers left to collect the remaining tablets. King Shrailzhar could rule Trilleah forever and all time without anyone disturbing him—or his groaning Forest of Waiting Ones—again.

Looking Back

Every mind was turning and spinning, but nobody was speaking about the things they were pondering. Some were thinking of family back home and wondered if they'd ever see them again. Others were considering the stolen souls of the loved ones caught in the forest, and who might come to Trilleah to finish what the Travelers had started. Would anyone know about the clay tablets and how many they still needed? Or about the Living Maps, which had seemingly failed them so badly today?

The new Travelers were thinking of the old Travelers, and the old Travelers were wondering about the new ones. Jennifer thought about none of these things. There was one thing on her mind, and not even the setting sun was going to distract her. That one thing was going to lead them out of the Labyrinth. She was concentrating on listening to whatever it was that was deep within her—her spirit, she supposed—so that she didn't miss even the smallest instruction. After many paths opening before her eyes, she had no doubt—not even a shred or a sliver—that something incredible had come to lead them out.

"I am NOT the leader," she wanted to scream to Miriam through her dreadfully scorched lips. Even though it looked to the others as though she was the leader, Jennifer knew she was not.

One turn after another after another after another and a light began to peek through the walled trees.

Just ahead. We are nearly there. Jennifer tried to shout out, "*LOOK!*" and pointed up ahead. She was disheartened when still no sound rolled off her tongue.

Nobody heard her silence, so nobody saw the light ahead. She forced her tired legs to move faster and faster until she was in a full run. Jennifer was tripping over her cloak and stumbling over the rough ground, but she didn't care. If she had to fall out of the Labyrinth, out of breath and completely spent, at least she—and the others—would be out. They would be back in the dark shadowy land of Trilleah, but certainly nothing out there could be as bad as what was inside the Labyrinth.

There may have been no movement from the king, but Jennifer had seen the dark beasts trying to sink their slime-covered teeth into the Travelers' flesh. She was thankful for the bubble of protection that had been spread over them, even if she was the only one who'd seen it. But none of that seemed to matter. Perhaps the bubble had kept out the grotesque flying creatures, but it had not kept out Miriam—the most evil beast Jennifer could imagine.

Her cheek stung. Her lips ached. She felt as if she was going crazy; quite crazy; maybe she was.

A few more steps and Jennifer lunged out of the Labyrinth. Miriam stepped over her, but Bella tripped and fell beside her. One by one as they exited the Labyrinth, they stumbled on the growing pile of Travelers laying on the ground. Some laughed, some cried, others kissed the ground, and still others spun and danced in the open air.

"It's very odd," Sam said, "that we're so happy to be back in the open air of such a horrible place."

"Isn't it," Matt said. Even Pierce was uncharacteristically excited, and as he ruffled up Sam's unruly mop of hair, he added a bunch of mumbo-jumbo that nobody understood. It was very unlike Pierce.

Jennifer wanted to add something as well, but she was afraid—afraid that she'd open her mouth and nothing would come out. She'd tried many times in the Labyrinth to speak and now, having been spit out of its foul grip, she hoped her voice would return. Regardless, she was afraid to try.

"We've got to hurry," Bella screeched. She stood up. Quickly, everyone was brought back to the importance of getting to the hollow.

"But we haven't found a tablet," someone cried.

"No, we have not," Bella said. "But if we don't get back to the hollow before the sun sets, we will have no need for any more tablets … ever!"

"How do we return to our hollow with the Labyrinth blocking us?" came the obvious question from a new and charming Traveler who identified herself as Tahlia.

As they pondered and looked at each other, a loud squeal came from Sam.

"LOOK!" he shouted. They spun around to see where he was pointing. Sure enough, the Labyrinth was gone—completely vanished into thin air. The gasp that arose from the group was deafening; it surely shook the Forest of Waiting Ones. That gasp echoed and was the only sound heard for quite some time. Every Traveler was so stunned that all words froze in their throats; none would come out of their mouths.

Even more disturbing, quite frankly, than the Labyrinth's disappearance, was the fact that the Malleana Forest was only a few feet away. They'd been walking for hours, most of the day in fact, in the enormous Labyrinth and yet once it was removed, they saw that they had gone only a very short distance.

Their minds were certainly a mess; like a puzzle box that had been shaken and broken up, their minds were shaken and greatly disturbed.

"How …" Matt finally mumbled.

"What …" Sam said.

"B-b-b-but," Bella stuttered. On and on it went. Nobody was making any more sense than anyone else, but all knew what the other meant. They were so close to the forest that the horrible groaning of the trees pierced their ears and broke their hearts.

Out of the Labyrinth and no longer in single file, they could finally see each other clearly. They began to look around, the old group of Travelers taking in the sights of the new group, and the new group getting a good look at the old group. There must have been six or seven who were new. Even if they had been to Trilleah before, they were new to Bella and Pierce, Matt, Sam, Judah, and Jennifer.

Kaija Mae still seemed to be the one in charge, although a little less now. She, too, had little to say at the moment. A very handsome young man, perhaps fourteen or fifteen years old, was looking intently at Jennifer, which made her uncomfortable. She could feel him staring at her, and she did everything she could to not stare back; he was very handsome.

"What happened to your cheek?" this handsome, nameless boy finally asked. Oh dear. That was one question—one of many—she was hoping no one would ask. Jennifer brought her hand up to touch the swollen mark at the same time both Bella and Pierce turned to look at it. Bella drew her breath in and took a step toward Jennifer.

"J," she shrieked, "what happened?"

"And your lips?" Matt shouted. "What happened to your lips?"

Jennifer looked at Miriam and opened her mouth to speak. As she did, the words of Miriam invaded her mind; *do not speak of this*, she remembered being whispered. Jennifer did begin to speak, silently praying for words to come out of her mouth. She began to tell what had happened, but as she did, the words on her tongue transformed into something she didn't have any thought of until they were lingering in the air.

"I ran into a tree," were the words that exited her mouth, although certainly not the ones she'd meant to speak.

Still looking at Miriam, Jennifer noticed that the evil traitor gave her a bit of a nod, a grin with no sign of any yellow or forked-tongue, and a wink.

Again, Jennifer tried to say what was on her mind and tell the others what had happened. Again as she opened her mouth, something different than what she had intended, pranced out.

"It was so dark," she heard herself say, "and I tripped a couple of times, I guess. I must have bumped into some sharp—hopefully not poisonous—thistles."

How is this happening? her mind screamed. Again the words of Miriam lingered.

Do not speak of this, jumped around in her mind, and she realized then, somehow, that Miriam had cast some miserably incomprehensible hex on her tongue. When she had touched Jennifer's lips and commanded that she not speak of what had happened, Jennifer's tongue somehow heard the command and had become, quite literally, unable to speak of it.

Reptilian Mindbenders

thirty one

Miriam, it turned out, was a Reptilian Mindbender. There would be nothing Jennifer could do to undo what Miriam had done, but because she had no knowledge of Reptilians or Mindbenders, she continued to try, nevertheless, becoming frustrated, angry, and fearful.

The more she tried to tell what had happened, the more elaborate the made-up story became on the thistles and tripping and getting punctured by them. Miriam looked pleased with herself. A smug look spread across her face and as it did, Jennifer again felt hot tears rush to the surface. In an attempt to distract all the eyes that were staring at her, she diverted the attention back to the forest and the vanishing Labyrinth.

"What now?" she asked. For the first time since Miriam had touched her lips, the words Jennifer had sent through them were actually the ones that came out. For the first time in a long time, someone else spoke up with a welcome answer.

"We follow the maps," Pierce said. "Now that the Labyrinth is gone, wherever it went, the path on the map makes sense."

"Let's go." Bella hollered. "Quickly."

Jennifer was relieved that she finally could fall back somewhere into the middle of the group; she moved in close beside Judah. She grabbed his hand and squeezed his fingers tightly, causing him to look at her.

Even though no words were spoken, Judah saw in her eyes that something had happened.

He would find out soon enough what that something was, but he knew his sister well enough to know that now was not the time, for she was struggling hard not to cry. He could see tears brimming in the corners of Jennifer's eyes, threatening to be unleashed and overflow. Judah knew better than to ask questions right now. He held her hand tightly and squeezed it a little—enough to let her know that he knew something had happened. That was all she could hope for right now.

They moved in quick step—Travelers ahead and Travelers behind—for a short amount of time. Pierce stopped and pulled two Living Maps from his cloak; he sprawled them out on the ground. There was no time for waiting of any kind. However, wait they must for there was no hurrying with the maps.

Those maps took an extra long time—in this exact moment when there was no extra time to be had. The Labyrinth was not on either of the maps, but the forest was. The maps couldn't seem to decide what to show the Travelers this time.

"They seem mixed up … or … or … confused maybe," Pierce whispered to Bella.

His whisper was too loud and everyone heard the words he meant for only Bella's ears. Either he was louder than he expected to be or the stiff breeze had snatched his words and carried them to unintended ears. Finally, another word was spoken.

"There," Bella said, her finger pointing at something on the maps.

"Yes. Yes, I see," Pierce screeched. He began to fold up the maps and everyone was relieved to see how they folded up easily and were satisfied to return to the inside of Pierce's cloak. The maps could be downright annoying sometimes when they had something to show.

While everyone was watching the maps, Jennifer was looking at something else far more intriguing. She was looking at Miriam. Normally, when Pierce laid out a map, Miriam would be right there, edging her way in to glance at it.

Not this time.

This time, she'd moved into the center of the new group of Travelers and was busily chatting away as though she didn't care at all about the maps or the path or the tablets. Jennifer's curiosity stirred, and she moved closer. She was very careful, though, because she did not wish to risk being seen by Miriam.

Judah continued to hold tightly to her hand, so Jennifer couldn't get close enough to hear what Miriam was saying. She considered letting go of her brother's hand and taking a few more steps, but just as she thought that would be a terrible idea, it stopped mattering one way or the other. As Jennifer was deciding what to do, Bella spoke up.

"The maps have shown the path … let's go!"

"What maps?" Voices from the new group of Travelers chimed in together, asking the question. That's when Miriam was heard loud and clear.

"You don't know about the maps?" she asked. "How have you gotten anywhere in Trilleah without the maps?"

Sam's rambling questions fit neatly between Miriam's.

"Do you have any tablets? How do you know where to go? Where is your hollow?" he asked. From hushed whispers to loud shouting, all of a sudden it seemed as though everyone wanted to know everything about everyone else. Questions and answers were exchanged so quickly that it was confusing to know who was the asker and who was the answerer.

Then, louder than all the ruckus that had suddenly erupted, came the most necessary and exciting and fearful question of them all. Matt was the one who gently opened his mouth and kindly, but firmly, asked it.

"If you have some tablets, and we have some tablets, perhaps together we have enough to break the curse of the Trows."

Silence. Every mouth sealed itself up, and every eye darted to Matt. Nobody, it seemed, knew what to say and so that is precisely what they said. Nothing. The anticipation of the answer—the possibilities of what it may mean—was nearly too much for them to consider.

"Well?" Matt broke the awkward silence. "Is that such an absurd thought?"

"Not at all," Tahlia—as she'd introduced herself earlier—replied. "We had four tablets collected." Then the handsome boy who Jennifer had noticed staring at her earlier, spoke up. Oh, he had such a wonderfully deep voice. The sound of it made Jennifer feel giggly. The words that swirled from his mouth, however, stopped her giggles instantly.

"Yes, we HAD four tablets, Tahlia!" Then he looked directly at Miriam and added, "They were stolen straight out of our hollow. Oh, I'm Aviel. Aviel Marlow."

Matt shook Aviel's hand, but it was Pierce who asked the questions. "Your tablets were stolen? How can that be? Where is your hollow that anyone could get in while you were gone?"

Jennifer thought to herself, *Pierce, you are not one bit interested in Aviel, or their stolen tablets; you just want to know so ours don't get stolen.* This was the truth of course, but as Jennifer kept thinking, she decided she was quite alright with Pierce's concern, even if it was for the wrong reasons.

Whatever his reasons for inquiring of Aviel, it didn't matter, because she too was suddenly concerned with the basket of clay tablets on their own eating stump in their own hollow. She wanted to rush straightaway to the hollow to ensure their safety.

Her mind fluttered back to when she'd arrived at the hollow earlier this morning. Her memory reminded her that she had stumbled upon Miriam having many of them in her hand and furthermore, the look on Miriam's face when Jennifer caught her, seemed to be that of a thief.

Bella interrupted everyone's thoughts, which was probably a good thing because nobody's thoughts were heading in a great direction.

"Hey! We have GOT to get moving." She sounded angry. "I feel terrible that your tablets were stolen, but ours were not. We have to find the tablet we came here to find, and we must do it NOW! The sun is moving quickly and our time is short. Please." she begged. "Let's get moving." Bella looked at Pierce, and immediately his questions stopped and his feet started.

"I'm sorry, Bella. You're right. Follow me." He waved his arms to make sure he had everyone's attention. Pierce turned and began running where there was no path, just to the west of Malleana Forest. It felt like the wrong way, but the maps had laid out their path clearly, and so, feelings had nothing to do with it, although it did seem to take a lot more faith in the maps now that they had just gone through the Labyrinth, of which the maps confusingly failed to be aware of, or so it seemed.

Jennifer realized she still had a firm grip on Judah's hand, and she considered letting go but decided it wasn't hurting anybody, so she hung on. Judah didn't seem to mind. Sometimes her brother could be such an annoyance and then other times, like now, he was a hero in her mind.

As they followed Pierce, not much thinking was required, so the travelers' thoughts took journeys of their own, wandering this way and that, mostly to home and the safety they knew would be found there—if they could get back. Some minds wandered to the missing tablets, but not Jennifer's. While her feet were very careful to follow behind Bella's, her mind took a journey of another sort, and she dreadfully pondered her burning lips and stinging cheek.

Would she ever be able to tell the others of Mariam and what she'd done?

Maybe back in the hollow, I'll be able to speak the words that are on my tongue, she hoped. *But if not there, then maybe it will be once we get back home and are safely in Westlock. When Miriam is nowhere to be found, I'll be able to tell Bella and Judah what happened. Surely, back home, she will lose her power to change my words. Please,* she begged, although, she was completely unsure to whom it was that she was begging. Simeon heard her and in his usual way, answered her gently.

Hush now, Little One, I am with you. A small grin snuck over Jennifer's lips, but as soon as it did, the stinging pain reminded her of Miriam's cruel finger touching her. *It's OK, Jenny, trust me.* But it was not OK in Jennifer's mind. Not even a little bit OK, and she let Simeon know of her displeasure.

How can you tell me it's OK? she thought harshly under her breath. *Were you there, Simeon? Did you see Miriam bite me? Did you see her snake tongue? Did you see her touch me and burn my lips? Did you?*

I saw, she heard faintly.

Then why did you let it happen? Again, her eyes filled with tears, and she wiped them away. *Why didn't you stop her?*

Jenny, you must understand. Even though I have the power to stop such a thing, sometimes it is better if I don't interfere. The tears in her eyes stopped coming because the painful sadness instantly turned to anger; tears don't come from anger.

Better? she snapped. *How can such a horrible thing be better than having that horrible thing not happen at all? HOW?*

She demanded an answer … but no answer came.

No Reasonable Solution

Jennifer was thankful that Judah was still holding her hand. She was furious with Simeon and listening hard to what ridiculous thing he could come up with to explain how letting Miriam hurt her was better than *not* letting Miriam hurt her.

Simeon, do not be silent now, she hollered without making a peep. *Don't you dare be silent now ...*

I'm not silent, Jenny; I am waiting for you to calm your anger before I answer so that you can hear my words and understand them. Anger is never a good state of mind to allow my voice to be heard correctly.

Fine, she screeched and took a deep breath, exhaling it through her nose, since even her own breath stung her lips. Another … and then one more. *OK, Simeon, I'm calm enough to hear you. Please, tell me how such a thing is better and if you could have stopped it from happening, why you didn't.*

Little One, he began, and even though his voice wasn't heard outside of her mind, she knew it was full of both compassion and sadness. *You needed to be aware that there is a Reptilian Mindbender among you. While she was able to cause you some pain, it's minor compared to what she is capable of if you were not aware of her presence,* Simeon explained. *You knew previously that she was a creature of Trilleah but had no proof of it; now you do. Now the others will believe you.*

That makes some sense, I suppose, she sighed. *But why me?* she asked. *And what, precisely, is a Reptilian Mindbender?*

Simeon answered straightaway. *It is because you believe that things are not what they appear. You believe you can see whatever is there to see and hear whatever is there to hear. The others do not believe as you do, limiting their abilities. But you,* he continued, *you have no doubt, and so you have a greater awareness of what is really there, just behind the veil of the air. It's all because you believe, Little One.*

You see this as a negative circumstance, but most sincerely I tell you it isn't negative at all. Sometimes Jennifer became so confused by Simeon that she wished she didn't hear him. *The ability to see such things gives you power over those things.* Again some anger was stirring in her, and she forced another few deep breaths in and out … in and out … before asking yet another question.

If I have so much power then why is it that MY cheek is bleeding, and MY lips are burned? Please, explain this to me, because it is hard for my tiny mind to understand such things.

Not now, Little One, you must trust me. Right now you must pay attention to your surroundings, for you are nearly to the tablet, and you MUST pay attention. Look, Jenny, with the eyes of your understanding. Forget not my words, for they will be your protection. And with that being said, which did nothing but confuse every corner of her already turbulent mind, Simeon fell silent.

WHAT ARE YOU TALKING ABOUT? she asked, but even while she made her mind scream the words, she knew they would go unanswered. She'd receive no more answers from her Shailma right now. He had said she must pay attention to her surroundings, so that was exactly what she decided to do.

Her eyes darted directly to Miriam and stayed there until Miriam saw her and shot a nasty glare right back. This time, however, instead of looking away Jennifer stared right back, determined to let this Reptilian Mindbender know that she was not afraid of her. It must have worked because not too many blinks were blinked before Miriam looked away. It struck Jennifer that Simeon had not told her what a Reptilian Mindbender was, but no matter, she'd ask him again later.

"There!" Pierce shrieked, pointing up ahead.

"What?" they wondered aloud because wherever "there" was that Pierce was shouting about, had not landed in the eyes of the rest.

"What are you talking about?" Sam blurted back.

"Where are you pointing?" asked Bella.

The new strangers asked similar questions. "I don't see anything different than two minutes ago," Kaija Mae announced.

Tahlia added the final question. "Um, where?"

"Oh, good grief," Pierce sighed. "Over there … past the last tree and over to the left half a turn." Although nobody saw what he was talking about yet, his description was good enough that it kept them busy looking for whatever was a "half a turn to the left of the last tree of the forest."

And then—and not all at once but here and there—voices were heard again.

"Oh!" hollered one.

"Mhm, I see it now," shrieked another.

"Good eye, Pierce," said Aviel in his wonderfully deep voice that made Jennifer's stomach tingle and jitter with all sorts of butterflies. Even though she had, like the rest, been busy looking, all Jennifer saw was a small space with tall weeds—or what looked like weeds. That patch of weeds could not be what they were all seeing, but there was nothing else noteworthy or different than they had been wandering in for the past twenty minutes, so the patch of weeds must have been what was so exciting, she supposed.

With just a few more steps, the Travelers walked right into the patch of weeds and for sure, they were nothing more than weeds. No significant space opened up in the sky, nor did the weeds part and make way for anything breathtaking to occur. It wasn't the weeds themselves, however, that they were looking for.

On just the other side of the weed patch, and indeed, they stood very tall in an attempt to hide what was meant to be seen, was a door in the side of a small hill. The door itself was no bigger than a hobbit door—or what one might assume the size of a hobbit door to be if ever there were such a thing. The slatted wooden door was not large enough for most of these Travelers to squeeze through, and of course, that caused concern for Jennifer, since she was by far the smallest of the Travelers. An even worse thought was that the next smallest Traveler was Miriam.

"No!" Jennifer said out loud, even though she meant for the word to stay quiet. Most everyone ignored her, except Judah, who looked directly at his sister and saw that whatever he'd seen in her eyes earlier was still there. Judah squeezed her hand firmly and gave her a telling nod.

"It's OK, Jelly Bean," he whispered as if he could read her thoughts … maybe he could. Maybe this was like one of their dreams where they both knew the same thing. Maybe Judah could see that her insides were in complete disarray.

"Jennifer," she heard Pierce say, "you are going to have to go in. I have no idea what's inside; let me lay out the second map and take a look."

At least there's a map for whatever lies behind this door, Jennifer thought, searching for anything to make this better. She felt many eyes staring at her, and looked up to catch Miriam's among them. It felt as though her glare was burning holes right through Jennifer's skin, causing her to wiggle unbearably inside of her cloak.

Again, Jennifer mustered up all her courage and begged Simeon to help her. Even though he was silent, she felt his presence strengthening her. Jennifer was able to lift her chin, straighten her back, think of Mamma, and stare down the Reptilian Mindbender for a second time.

It took a bit longer than last time to make Miriam look away, but Jennifer felt a small surge of confidence weave through her veins as she realized Miriam might have just shown the slightest bit of fear toward Jennifer. Perhaps "fear" was too strong of a word, but there was a weakness in Miriam that was peeking through; Jennifer took great delight in seeing it.

Pierce's voice rang out and pulled Jennifer's attention back to the reality before them.

"Come here, Jennifer, and look at this map," he said. He was tugging on her cloak and Jennifer realized that he'd already called her many times, but she'd been too preoccupied with Miriam to hear him.

She squatted down and began looking at the most amazing map she'd ever seen—even in her most outrageous imaginings. She sucked in her breath.

"You're a hollow," she whispered to the map.

Even though she'd not meant for anyone to hear her, Pierce had. He bent down and whispered back, "Yes, it is."

"Pierce, I'm afraid. I can't go in alone," she whispered, but even as she said the words, her mind heard the ever familiar and comforting voice of Simeon.

Jennifer, you know you're not alone.

She had no time to respond since Pierce and Bella were both tugging at her to look carefully at the living map, which was frantically opening up passageways and stumps and secret doors in every direction on the other side of the wooden door. The hollow seemed to go on forever. Just when it looked like the map was finished, a whole new section would open up, revealing more of the hollow.

"Oh dear," Jennifer mumbled and touched her burning lips. Suddenly, to make matters a thousand times worse, the pair of eyes that had been showing up back home—the ones that were somehow inside her mind and peering out through her own eyes—chose this moment to return. They'd come to peek through her eyes at the map.

Jennifer wondered if she shut her own eyes then maybe the intruding eyes would be unable to see it, but then again, she needed to see it herself. It was a horrible conundrum without any reasonable solution or possible answers.

Again, Jennifer was caught in a horrible dilemma of which only she was aware.

Secrets Within

thirty three

Jennifer wondered again if she should try to explain such a thing to Bella. As she pondered how to do so—because honestly, she couldn't understand such a thing herself—the eyes gave her a message. *Do not tell them I'm here. If you tell them I am here, I'll have to leave. They'll make me go. Do not tell them I'm here, Jennifer ... DO NOT tell them.*

Like so many other things she'd heard on this journey, the words didn't come through her ears. It was more like a knowing of some unexplainable sort—the same way she knew what the light in the Labyrinth wanted her to know.

Now Jennifer was at the fullest measure of both fear and confusion. There were too many things going on at once; it was overwhelming. But there was another feeling that was stirring; compassion. Compassion for whomever this was whose eyes were using her own as a window of sorts. This being did not want to be forced to leave and even though Jennifer couldn't determine who—or what—it was, she decided not to reveal its presence to Bella or Pierce. Not yet. What could it hurt to keep its secret?

"Finally," she heard a few voices squeal.

"What?" Jennifer replied. She had again, gotten distracted and taken her eyes off of the very thing they should have been on.

"The map is finished. Let's wait for the path to show itself, and then you can go get the tablet," someone said. Jennifer was so busy thinking, she never noticed who said the words.

"Oh, you make that sound easy," she whined. "Like I'm going to wander in and wander back out without any trouble at all!"

"J," Bella said, "you won't be alone."

Oh no, Jennifer thought. She already knew that they were going to try sending Miriam in with her, so she looked at Bella and said, "Judah must come with me. He's not too big to fit through the door."

Judah must have heard his name because he stepped up and said, "Am I going with Jelly Bean?"

"Yes! Yes, you are," she said and grabbed his hand again. Nobody said otherwise, and she was relieved. She was also relieved that the map had finally drawn the direction they were to go. It seemed they'd be required to go only a short distance, once inside the hollow.

This hollow looked a lot like their own, at least the layout, so it should be simple—through the Eating Chamber, to the far side, through a passageway, to the second secret door on the left.

"It's kind of like going from math to the science lab at school," Judah said. He chuckled, trying to make Jennifer less uptight, but everyone knew there was nothing to find amusing. The hollow didn't seem overwhelming, nor did the path where they'd go once inside. The problem was the three orange dots that had a glow to them. They were not all together, and they were moving in different directions.

"Are they more Travelers?" Bella asked of Pierce.

"I have no idea," he replied. No matter what he said or how kind he tried to speak, he always had an edginess to his voice that caused people to be unsure of him. Pierce always sounded perturbed no matter what the question, or who was asking it.

"I've been watching them, though," he said. "The path was undoubtedly working to avoid the orange dots."

"Well, that can't be a good thing," Jennifer said to nobody in particular.

Bella replied, trying to calm whatever might be stirring in her niece. "If you follow the map's path you'll be fine."

"Yes," Jennifer snarled, "because the map has never led us wrong before."

The only person who could speak to Jennifer in a way that she'd listen and believe at this point was Matt, so naturally, she was as pleased as she could be in such a drastic circumstance, when the hand on her arm belonged to him.

"Jennifer," he said calmly. "I've been thinking about that, and I don't think the map did mislead us." Everyone gathered to listen to his reasoning because it seemed, without a doubt whatsoever, that the map had misled them terribly.

"The map took us right here, right where we needed to be and, in fact, today's journey would have been a rather short, simple one if not for the Labyrinth."

"Yes," Sam spoke up. "That's right Matt, except" … and then Sam's voice got loud and his eyes got large as he finished his sentence. "The Labyrinth WAS there."

"Let me finish." Matt looked around the group and saw that every eye, both in their own group of Travelers and the group they'd come upon inside the Labyrinth, was glued to him as he explained. He took a breath and blew it out slowly before continuing.

"I believe that the Labyrinth was not there when the map drew its paths for us. I think that the perfidy of it was just that—it was a cunning plan King Shrailzhar created to appear after the map had laid out our plan."

"We all knew there was something strange about it when we first stepped into it. Do you recall? We wondered why this thing hadn't been on the map, and we questioned entering into it. It wasn't the maps that failed us, but we that failed ourselves. We should have taken a few minutes; opened the maps up and checked again. We know how quickly things can shift here in Trilleah, and when our hearts told us something wasn't right, we shouldn't have ignored them.

"Something else I pondered was this. There were others already caught in the perfidy of the Labyrinth, others that had no maps to lead them. Maybe we were supposed to enter the maze and find these Travelers. Otherwise, they may not have gotten out. Either way," Matt continued, looking around at those who were listening, "we didn't get trapped inside. The king failed to capture us and now, we are close to collecting another clay tablet."

While everyone was intently listening to Matt's ideas, nobody spoke. There was a few "mhm's" and "hmmm's," going on and a lot of considerings and a whole bunch of wonderings. Now that he seemed to be finished, Sam was the first to speak.

"Yup," was what he said. "That's what happened, alright."

Pierce took no care to mask his annoyance this time when he replied to Sam. "How do YOU know?" he barked.

"I just know. I can't tell you how. As soon as Matt started explaining, something in my belly said, 'listen; he's speaking the truth.'" Pierce just rolled his eyes and looked back to the orange dots on the map that still laid open on the ground.

"Pierce," Bella said, "so did mine. I heard similar words in my belly." Then, a few more joined in.

"So did I," said Aviel.

"Me too," chimed in Kaija Mae and Talia.

"So that seems to be the truth then, I guess," said Bella. "If Matt had the explanation and the rest of us—or most of us—had the same knowing in our bellies, then that must be the truth. At least, it would seem to me."

"Whatever," Pierce snapped back. It wasn't unlike him to snap at someone, but it was very unlike him to snap at Bella.

"The orange dots are still now. Look one more time at where you're to go—and take the map, I suppose." Pierce said. "In case you get inside and there's a change that we don't see now." Again he rolled his eyes, and Bella smacked him on the back.

"Pierce!" she said gruffly. "Stop now." He grinned at her but didn't say anything more about it. Instead, he turned and looked at Judah. "Ready?" he asked the boy.

"Ready," Judah replied, eager to get inside, but even more eager to get back out again. Jennifer was not eager, however, and whined fiercely.

"I'm not ready. I'll never be ready."

She would have continued her pity-party, but Pierce set one hand on the top of each of the twins' heads and said, "You'll be OK, and we'll be right here waiting." It was somewhat miraculous and spooky how Pierce could go back and forth between being a complete tyrant one minute and a compassionate friend the next.

"Go quickly," Bella said. She kissed them both on the cheeks and stepped out of the way, leaving nothing between the twins and the door. Jennifer looked at Judah … Judah looked back at Jennifer. Nobody said a word; everyone took a few steps back.

It was finally Judah who spoke up. "Let's do this thing, Jelly Bean."

And with those words, he squeezed her hand, stepped forward, and pushed open the tiny door. The twins hunched down and squeezed inside; the door slammed shut behind them with a loud thud.

And with that, they were gone.

The slam of the door echoed … Bella burst into tears.

"What are we doing?" she wailed. "They are so young, Pierce! We should have gone ourselves." Pierce, Matt, and Sam gathered around her. Pierce held onto her tightly; she buried her face in the shoulder of his cloak and continued to sob.

"Bella," Matt said, "there was no way any of the rest of us would have squeezed through that door. Judah barely made it inside."

"If I could have gone in I sure would have, Bella," Sam spouted. "I'm just too tall!"

Kaija Mae joined the chatter, trying to console Bella. "I haven't known you all for long. Well, I don't know you at all, I guess. But I know those two will be fine in there. For some reason, it was the two of them who had to go in—together. There's an important connection between the two of them—a connection that no one else in either of our groups has—that made it necessary that they are the ones to go into the hollow."

"I know, Kaija Mae!" Aviel said. He seemed rather delighted. "I felt the same way." He moved closer to Bella and the group of young men who'd gathered around her. "The moment I saw the odd, little door, I knew it was the two of them who would need to go inside. Honestly, I wasn't sure Judah would be able to squeeze through."

Bella had calmed enough to listen to their words. She began to believe them, slightly. "They're twins," she sniffled and wiped her nose with the back of her sleeve. "You know," Bella pondered out loud, "J said something to me earlier in our hollow. When we arrived in Trilleah, she mentioned that her Shailma had told her she'd have to rely on Judah completely—and Judah on her—for any of us to get out of Trilleah."

"Judah told me something similar, Bella," Matt mentioned quietly. "I don't know the reason, but I do know it's the twins who need to be in there and find the tablet."

"They'll be fine," Pierce said. Bella sniffled and continued to use the back of her sleeve to wipe the tears that were beginning to slow.

As the Travelers continued chattering on about the twins and the benefits of being here together, Judah and Jennifer were busily sneaking through the hollow, trying to remember which way they were to go. It was too dark to spread the map out, so they'd need to rely on their memories.

"Through the Eating Chamber to the far side, through a passageway, and the second secret door on the left," Judah repeated.

Even though they'd come to understand that maybe the maps had not led them wrong earlier—into the Labyrinth—they still had a hard time trusting the maps completely.

"Judah, there are three passageways on the far side of the Eating Chamber. Oh dear," she sighed. "I knew this wouldn't be as easy as the others said."

Judah took his sister's hand and squeezed it. "Jelly Bean," he sighed, "the map showed all three passageways, remember?" He didn't wait for her to answer because it didn't matter one iota if she remembered or not. "The path went into the one on the far left, so we'll take that one." He pointed to the smallest of the three passageways and headed toward it, tugging Jennifer behind him.

"Judah, I'm scared," she whispered.

"I know, Jelly Bean," Judah said. "I know."

There seemed to be no fear in his words, but Jennifer knew he must be scared—at least a little. They darted into the passageway outlined on the map and looked for the hidden door. Were all the passageways the same? Would the chambers here have the same kinds of hidden doors as in Asphelia's Hollow? It's quite difficult to look for something that could be invisible … very difficult indeed.

Something moved. In the dark corners, which were pretty much everywhere, something moved and both the twins were startled. There was no doubt about it. Both Jennifer and Judah froze. Neither spoke; not even a whisper.

It moved again. And again. In an instant, Judah shoved his sister against the opposite wall and stood in front of her, blocking her from whatever it was they knew to be lurking in the shadows. Loudly he raised his voice, an authority that did not sound even a little like Judah, carried his words.

"Who are you and what do you want with us?" he demanded.

"I AM CHOSHEK," came a voice so wretched it turned the air foul. The words hung in the air like crystals. As the name Choshek wafted from the shadowy corner, so did the most horrendous looking beast that even the most outrageous imagination would be unable to consider. This monster consisted of a black skull with holes for eyes, but where no eyes rested. It had no nose but instead, a large spiraled horn protruded where a nose should be. It had no lips. Nothing covered the brown, razor-sharp teeth—if one might call them teeth—dripping with a dark green liquid. Truly, Choshek was the most grotesque creature one would ever be forced to lay eyes on, and here it was, hunched over, yet still towering three feet above the twins.

Jennifer could only see a small part of the beast since Judah made very sure to stand in her way, or Choshek's way perhaps, to block one from the other.

"You will not pass this way," the evil voice gurgled. As his words clawed their way through the foul air and slammed into the twin's ears, Choshek took a step toward them, blocking the passageway completely. He raised a sword so sharp that it sliced the air between them, opening a tiny gap into some other world; one their eyes hadn't noticed before, but one they couldn't ignore now.

Neither Judah nor Jennifer wanted to consider that there might be a whole other world than the one to where they wanted to return or this one of Trilleah, from which they desperately wanted to escape. However, it did seem that another world altogether different was peeking through the air where his sword had pierced the darkness. Choshek held the sword with one hand while he swiped the other through the air, closing the gap he'd made … but not soon enough to delete it from either of the twin's minds.

Jennifer could not take any more. Fear grabbed her and she fainted, falling hard to the floor and smashing her head into the ground with a loud "thud." She neither saw, nor heard, anything else that went on between Judah and Choshek in that cave on that day. Jennifer would never know how Judah stood up to such an evil-hearted beast … but indeed, he did.

Judah jumped, startled by the sound of his sister's head thumping against the hard floor. He turned briefly to see what had happened and a small pool of blood caught his eye. Judah balled up his fists tightly and gritted his teeth hard to keep from crumbling into a pile of uselessness himself. He whispered through his teeth without moving his mouth.

"Jelly Bean," Judah whispered as loud as possible. He got no reply.

"Shemaiah," he called. "Shemaiah, help me!" he hollered, trying to keep the words inside his hood. When Choshek responded, Judah knew he had been louder than he'd intended and the words had spilled out of his hood. Fear gripped him and he froze.

Of Battle & Blood

thirty five

"Ha Ha Ha," the towering beast sneered. As he did, sludge spewed everywhere, covering Judah. "Do NOT tell me that you believe in such things as Shailmas!" He threw his head back, laughing hysterically. A putrid smell came from Choshek as he both roared and snarled at the same time. "Oh no … NO, no, no you cannot believe in such fairy tales." He continued his taunting and laughing, and Judah was oddly thankful. At least in these few moments,

Choshek had become so preoccupied with himself that he failed to notice Judah slowly kneel down beside his sister. He was trying to find the source of all the blood that was coming from her.

It wasn't too hard to find. As Judah kept one eye on Choshek, he rolled Jennifer over and noticed immediately the deep gash that had spread itself thick just behind her right ear.

"Oh Jelly Bean," Judah gasped. As he put his hand over the harsh wound to try and stop the bleeding, he looked up to see Choshek had stopped laughing and had noticed Jennifer.

Choshek lowered his sword slightly and took a couple of steps toward the twins. "Oh, how I've been waiting for the blood of that girl," the beast sneered. "King Shrailzhar promised her blood to me long ago; I have been waiting for this day." Choshek began spitting a grayish-brown foam and took another step toward the twins.

With one quick swing of his arm, Judah ripped his cloak up over his head and spread it swiftly over his sister. "Hold on, Jelly Bean," he whispered. Rage toward the beast filled him up.

As Judah tossed his cloak over Jennifer, Shemaiah heard his cries and answered. Immediately, Shemaiah told Judah to put his cloak back on. He listened, and even though Judah wanted to keep his sister covered, he knew that his Shailma must have a reason for such instructions.

Judah, the Shailma whispered to his heart, *I am here. I will keep you, do not be afraid. I am surrounding you; I am before you and behind you. I will hedge you in. You have nothing to fear, my dear boy.*

Even though not much of what Shemaiah was saying made sense, Judah knew well enough that all he really needed to understand was that his Shailma was with him. The boy would do whatever was required, even if it seemed outrageously crazy. Quicker than lightning strikes, Judah's mind went back to his entry into Trilleah.

"Do you trust me?" Shemaiah had asked just before turning and racing headlong into the countless warriors in King Shrailzhar's army. Even though it appeared to Judah as though he'd be captured and added to the Forest of Waiting Ones, Shemaiah knew better. He heard the same question now being asked of him again, deep in his heart.

Do you trust me?

You know I trust you, Judah responded, even though fear burrowed through his flesh and clawed at his heart. *But if only one of us can be saved, save my sister,* he added when he saw the vast amount of blood pooling on the floor.

Judah, Shemaiah spoke. *Feel into the right pocket of your cloak with your left hand.* Judah did as he was instructed, and his hand grasped something cold and smooth; something he'd never felt in his cloak before.

As Judah painstakingly listened and did everything Shemaiah was saying, he did not take his eyes off Choshek, for the hideous beast was still moving toward Jennifer, the sour foam now bubbling and spilling onto the floor. Judah did not move from the side of his unconscious sister.

Shemaiah directed him to now throw the cloak over his sister and stand up solid, raising his left arm high, grasping tightly to what he'd found in the pocket of his cloak. Judah did so, but a dark terror made his legs wobble as he threw the cloak over Jennifer and stood. In protecting her, he suddenly realized that he was completely unprotected ... or so he thought.

As Judah obeyed his Shailma, the boy grew in strength, and as Choshek took more steps toward the twins, Judah carried out the final order of Shemaiah. He raised his left arm. Whatever had been hiding in his cloak suddenly became unbearably heavy and Judah had to add his right hand to grab it quickly before it came crashing down on himself.

Judah briefly directed his eyes from Choshek to see what he was holding above his head and nearly fell over when he realized what he was grasping. Above his head, held firmly between both his hands, was the biggest sword Judah had ever seen. No wonder it was so heavy. As he felt incredibly powerful with such a sword, the feeling quickly faded when he realized he had no idea how to use such a mighty weapon. He barely had the strength to hold it upright; he certainly did not have the strength to swing it fiercely and overtake Choshek.

Do not worry yourself, Judah, Shemaiah whispered. *I know how to use it full well. Even though you are holding onto the sword, I assure you, son, both you and the sword are in MY hands.*

Judah was gravely confused, but with all his strength he raised the heavy sword high above his head and said the only thing he could say. *OK Shemaiah, I trust you.* That was all he could do, but seemingly, it was all that was required. As soon as he spoke the words, Judah felt a power come into the sword and down into his hands and arms, spreading throughout his entire self—a power that was most certainly not his own.

The sword-wielding boy stepped forward—right in front of Choshek—and a most vicious battle ensued. The sound of metal against metal clashed loudly, vibrating and echoing inside the small, dimly-lit chamber. It was so loud that Judah was sure his sister would be startled back into consciousness at any moment. She wasn't.

He tried to keep an eye on her but found it impossible as the onslaught of the battle progressed. The worst thing that could happen, in his mind, was for Jennifer to gain consciousness again in the middle of the fight. Now he found himself hoping she would remain exactly where she was.

*** CLANG *** BASH *** CLANG *** CLANG *** BASH

The battle continued back and forth, back and forth; thunderous and deafening as blade struck against heavy blade. Judah's arms were getting too tired to continue much longer. Even if it was Shemaiah who was wielding the sword, Judah was still the one holding it up and it was becoming unbearable.

Shemaiah could sense his exhaustion and before long, Judah heard the voice of his Shailma deep in his own heart. *Judah—life is in the blood. For Choshek, however, Jennifer's lifeblood will be his death blow.*

"WHAT?" Judah screamed out in the midst of the battle. The voice in his heart was faint and even though it was inside of his mind, the sound of heavy clashing swords was too loud for him to hear it clearly. Shemaiah repeated the words, this time so loudly that Judah was sure the Shailma's voice had been trumpeted directly into his ears.

"Jennifer's lifeblood will be Choshek's death blow."

For the brief moments it took to hear the words, and the ones that followed, every other sound in that chamber became silent to Judah.

Choshek is defeated not by the sword, but by the blood. Judah did not know what that meant, but it did not sound good. He was hoping to keep all his blood inside of his body.

"I'm not sure how that helps me, Shemaiah," Judah screamed.

Choshek will lose his sword—briefly. Precisely at that moment, you must hurry and dip your sword into Jennifer's blood that has spilled onto the ground. Judah was trying to follow these instructions, but they seemed far too outrageous; he questioned whether he'd heard correctly at all, or if it was the terror of the moment that was causing him to think such ridiculous things.

When you do, Choshek will have time to regain his sword. Judah, you must follow my instructions with exact precision—and speedily—both you and Jennifer's lives depend on it. Judah listened more intently and was fully determined to do what Shemaiah said.

When Choshek has his sword back, you must run with all the strength you have left, directly toward him. I will help you.

This was too much for Judah to take in, but he focused on Shemaiah's words, repeating them over and over under his breath all the while the swords continued to bash and clang against one another.

At the last second, when you think you don't have enough strength for one more step, force your legs to take one more step anyway. When you do, lower your sword. You will merely be able to prick Choshek, but because his defeat is in the blood and not in the sword, you will gain the victory.

Judah didn't think he had the strength for one more step even now, so how was he going to find enough strength to follow through on all Shemaiah's instructions? He was overwhelmed by it all. He had no answer. He did the only thing he could do; he asked for help.

"Shemaiah, I'm too tired. If my arms were not throbbing, I fear I'd not feel them at all!" he shouted. "I cannot do this without your strength and your power and your might. If you promise to be with me, then I will carry on. I need your help."

I promise you, my son, were the last words that came from Shemaiah before Judah watched Choshek's sword fly from his grip. Judah was suddenly flooded with a new measure of strength and courage. He spun around and sliced the blade of the sword through the dirt floor in front of his sister where her blood had spilled out—just as Shemaiah had instructed him. As he lifted the bloody blade back into the air, many drops of Jennifer's blood fell, landing on Judah's cheek. He felt sudden panic as the drops ran down his face, not knowing if his sister would ever recover.

Judah looked back toward Choshek and just as Shemaiah had said, the evil demon had retrieved his sword and was coming toward Judah hard and fast, laughing and spewing putrid sludge all around. A shiver surrounded Judah and held him close—too close. Regardless, he lowered the sword slightly, and with every morsel of strength he had remaining, he ran toward Choshek, screaming his sister's name.

"FOR JENNIFER," bounced from one stone wall to another and back again. It was deafening.

At the last possible moment, Judah lowered his sword more so the blood-covered blade went slightly into Choshek's belly. It did not go through him as Judah had hoped, but just a small prick was made; barely noticeable. At first, the disgusting beast did not flinch and Judah panicked. Maybe it wasn't enough. Maybe Choshek wasn't beaten by the blood after all! But within seconds he slowed, and with one filthy, clawed hand, he grabbed his belly.

True to the words of Shemaiah, despite how tiny the wound, Choshek dropped his sword. He fell to his knees and tried desperately to claw the blood out of the small wound. And then, a scream louder than Judah had ever heard before exited Choshek's throat, echoing all around the chamber. It was so strong that Judah thought—just for a second—that he could see the scream bounce from wall to wall to wall.

And then … silence.

Choshek slumped to the floor. He faded until he had completely evaporated into the air, leaving nothing more than a putrid green fog. All that remained of the horrific beast was his sword, a bit of brown sludge that ran down the stone walls, and the putrid smell still lingering in the air.

"Pick up his sword, Judah," came the calm words of Shemaiah into the wretched hollow. Judah instantly followed the instruction. "Throw it into the fire." These instructions made no sense because Judah had not seen any fire. Nevertheless, he looked around, trusting his Shailma now more than ever.

Judah searched the chamber one way and then another and sure enough, at the far end of one of the passageways, close to where they had entered, a very small flicker caught his eye.

He bent over to pick up Choshek's sword and found it to be a hundred times heavier than the one he had been using himself.

Judah set his own down and wrapped both hands around the gigantic handle of Choshek's sword. There was no way he was going to be able to pick it up. Instead, he dragged it down the chamber toward the fire. The razor-sharp blade made a horrible screeching sound and forged a deep crevasse in the dirt floor behind him. It took more strength than the boy had, but he knew Shemaiah was lending him all the strength required.

By the time Judah reached the fire, the blaze had become enormous. He could not lift the sword, so he dragged it into the fire. Just before he was about to let it go, he heard Shemaiah's voice.

"Judah, hold onto it. Do not let it drop into the fire." Judah held on.

"Shemaiah, it's getting too hot!" he cried out.

"Hold on just a little longer, Judah," his Shailma urged. Just about the time Judah thought he could not hold on any longer and was about to let go, a dark orange smoke billowed out of the fire and the blade of the sword fell away and was burned up. The handle —so horribly hot it had burned his flesh—turned to ash, falling like sand through his fingers, and leaving something cold against his burned skin. As Judah stepped away from the fire, he immediately recognized what was left behind; what had been hidden inside the handle of Choshek's battle sword.

Muffled Silence

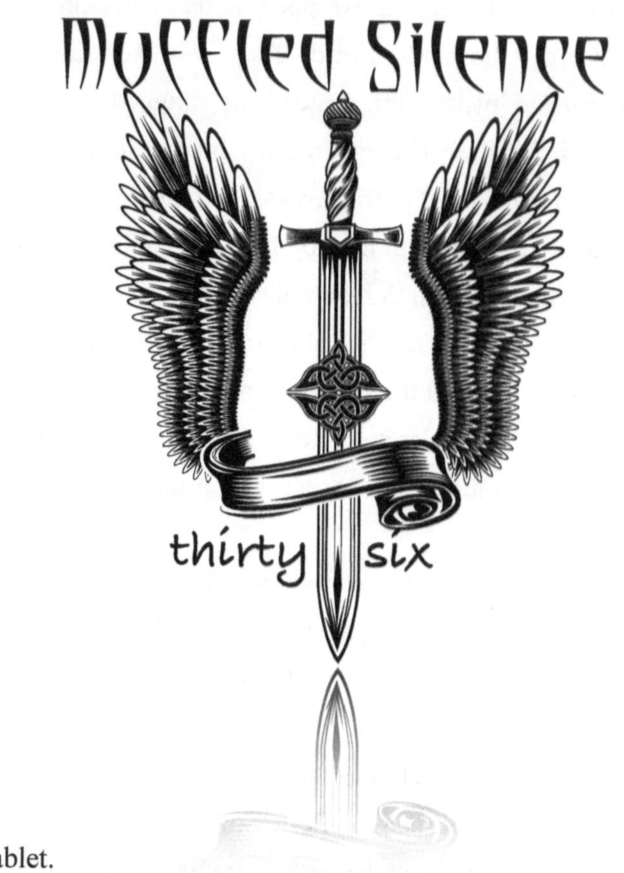

A tablet.

The clay tablet they had entered this hollow to find, was now cradled in Judah's burned hands, and he was dumbfounded.

"How … what … but …" Judah could not find words to make any sense or ask the question he wanted to ask. He didn't even know which question to start with. The boy just stood there for a long moment mumbling nonsense and turning the tablet over and over. His hands, though burned, felt no pain, for too many other feelings overwhelmed him. He felt it and looked at it and tried to read the words on the tablet but, of course, he was unable to do so.

Judah ... Judah ...

The voice in his mind that had been begging for his attention finally got it. Shemaiah had been calling his name for quite some time, trying to hurry him along. Finally, Judah shook his head, still in disbelief at what he held in his hands, but ready to hear Shemaiah's instructions.

Judah, time is running out. The sun is setting.

Suddenly, Judah remembered where he was ... and where his sister was. He shoved the clay tablet deep into the pocket of his pants, since his cloak was still covering Jennifer. Judah ran back down the chamber to find her still lying just as she'd fallen. He scooped up his cloak and threw it over his shoulders.

For no particular reason he knew of, his fingers found the clay tablet and he quickly moved it from his pants pocket to the inside pocket of his cloak. Judah knew for certain that it would not fall out if his cloak held onto it.

He knelt down and looked again at his sister's head. The bleeding had stopped, but her eyes remained closed. The hard ground had drunk in Jennifer's blood that had poured out earlier, leaving nothing more than a dark stain in the dirt. Judah, his hands shaking and throbbing fiercely now, hung them in front of his sister's pale face, hoping and praying he'd feel her breath.

He did.

Judah let out a sigh of relief, aware that he had been holding his breath since he'd knelt down. He carefully wiggled one arm under Jennifer's head and the other under her knees, cringing from the pain of his burned hands but knowing the pain didn't matter. Judah forgot that his arms were weary from the task of the sword, and lifted Jennifer.

"Let's go, Jelly Bean," he whispered and lightly kissed her bloody cheek. "Our job here is done; the tablet has been found."

He turned to go back down the chamber he'd just run through and noticed the deep crevice Choshek's sword had left in the dirt. He decided he wanted no sign of that dreadful beast to remain and began kicking up the dirt as he walked, half-dragging his feet and half-kicking at it.

Judah, Shemaiah urged, *there's no time for such foolishness. Just go.*

Go he did.

In only a few more strides he reached the opening where moments ago the fire—which had disintegrated Choshek's sword—had roared wildly. Now, it was barely more than a smoldering pile of ashes. With one long stride, he stepped over it. Moments later, he exited through the tiny hollow door and back into the stale air of Trilleah.

The first to see them was Bella, who reacted with a loud scream.

"Jennifer!" she wailed and moved closer to see her niece's bloody face. "What happened?" she whispered, overcome with grief.

Matt was alarmed by Bella's shrieks. He moved in close and carefully took Jennifer from Judah's tired arms. The sight of the twins caused every Traveler to begin asking a thousand questions, all hurriedly gathering around them.

Judah was overwhelmed.

He pushed his way out of the crowd, but as he stomped past Bella, he thrust his hand deep into the pocket that held the precious tablet and angrily shoved it toward her.

"I believe this is what we needed," he said, emotion welling up inside his belly.

All at once, the mumbling gibberish of the Travelers came to a halt, and silence passed between them.

"We must go," Judah snapped. "I'll tell you what happened later, but for now, the sun is nearly gone."

"Yes," Bella said.

"Hurry," Kaija Mae added. It seemed to Judah that while the twins had been inside the hollow, fighting for their lives, the two groups of Travelers had merged and were now all mixed amongst each other. Kaija Mae walked with Bella; Aviel hurried alongside Matt, helping to carry Jennifer.

Nothing more was said as the Travelers hurried through the Forest of Waiting Ones, and it seemed, at least to Judah, that the moaning of the trees was noticeably quieter than usual. He wondered why, but somehow he already knew. They were all watching Jennifer, listening … waiting … hoping. Suddenly his stomach became wretched, and he threw up at the side of the path.

They're waiting to see if the Trows will steal Jennifer's soul. His ears heard the words, but he didn't know from where they had come. Was it Shemaiah? It wasn't a voice heard in his heart, but more heard with his ears and Shemaiah didn't speak to his ears out in the open like this, where someone else might hear.

Judah looked around to see if anyone was watching him, hoping it was one of the Travelers who spoke the words, but no one was even glancing in his direction.

As he turned his head back to the path, one Traveler did catch his eye and he felt uncomfortable with what he saw. Miriam seemed to be looking back and forth between him and Jennifer.

Her gaze seemed to land heavily on Jennifer, however, and a deep uneasiness welled up in Judah.

I will keep my eye on that one, he thought. At the same time that he thought the thought, his eyes caught was seemed to be something in Miriam's mouth.

Couldn't be, he said to himself and let the curiosity quietly dissolve.

As was always the case when one of the Travelers had a private thought that was responded to unexpectedly by their Shailmas, Judah was startled.

Shemaiah had heard his thoughts and had returned a response.

You had better keep an eye on that one, was the thought dropped into Judah's belly.

Yes ... you had better.

Last Sliver of Sun

Pondering such a deep and bothersome thought, Judah hurried to move alongside Matt and Aviel, who were quickly ducking and weaving to maneuver Jennifer through the forest. He unbuttoned his cloak and began to remove it; Bella noticed what he was doing.

"Judah, NO!" she said. "You mustn't."

"Bella, I have to," he replied firmly but in a hushed under-his-breath sort of way. "The Trows are watching her—watching and waiting—and I would rather be uncovered than have Jennifer be seen in her broken state." Kaija Mae fell into step between Judah and Bella. She began to agree with Bella, but Judah stopped them both. "She's an easy target for the Trows, and I will not have my sister become part of the Forest of Waiting Ones. It's my job to cover her … even if that means being uncovering myself. So be it," he sighed.

Neither of the girls could argue with his reasoning, so Judah continued to remove his cloak and cover his sister. She was still wearing her own cloak but just to be certain, Judah felt it best to lay his cloak over her as well. He glanced over to Miriam as he did and saw that her eyes were fixed on Jennifer; like a wolf eyeing its prey.

Judah kept looking at Miriam, hoping she would notice and look back at him. He wanted to give her a look that would scream, "STAY AWAY FROM MY SISTER," but Miriam's eyes never once strayed from Jennifer.

"Besides," he added, moving his attention briefly back to Bella and Kaija Mae in one last effort to calm them, "we come through Malleana Forest every time we come to Trilleah, and we never have our cloaks until we get to the hollow."

That was a good point, and it calmed the girls dramatically. Judah couldn't tell them the truth—that he'd noticed Miriam staring at Jennifer—or that something had happened between his sister and Miriam earlier when his Jennifer's lips had been burned and her cheek had been pierced. Even though Judah had no idea *what* had occurred, he knew that *something* had by the look in Jennifer's eyes when she'd grabbed his hand earlier, back in the Labyrinth.

If she were merely Judah's sister, they likely would not have been able to understand each other's thoughts, actions, looks or unspoken words as clearly. However, because they were twins, Judah was very aware that the look in Jennifer's eyes back there, before she'd passed out, had to do with Miriam. He had no doubt that something grievous had occurred between the girls and was determined to find out what. Until he knew for sure though, he decided not to make any mention of it to the others.

Judah also remembered, now that he was thinking more clearly about it, that Jennifer seemed to be trying to tell him something, but her words would not come out. That was unusual for his sister, so he knew something horrible had happened to keep her from telling him about it. Judah suddenly became anxious to speak to his sister, and uneasy about Miriam's presence … and stares … and the strange tongue he was sure he'd seen earlier.

Now, watching Miriam as she watched Jennifer, seeing her eyes lose their color and noticing again that her tongue seemed all of a sudden somehow too big for her mouth, he knew covering Jennifer with his cloak was necessary, even if left him out in the open— exposed and an easy target. His thoughts went no farther; they were halted by a shriek coming from his aunt.

"There it is," Bella cried as she pointed with both hands to Asphelia's Hollow. "Straight ahead." There were shouts and hollers and cheers and whistles from the Travelers. Every one of them had been concerned they would not make it back in time to leave before the Solstice Gates were closed.

Even now, there was barely more than a sliver of a shadow of light being cast from the sun, as it was nearly finished its setting process. The Travelers picked up speed and began running toward the hollow.

"Where is your hollow?" Bella asked Kaija Mae.

"It is not far from here; another ten to fifteen minutes to the south."

"You don't have time to get there. Come to Asphelia's Hollow with us or you'll not escape Trilleah," Matt shouted to the others.

"Ya," Sam agreed, tripping over tree roots and unfamiliar rocks on the path. "You gotta come to our hollow so you can get home! Hurry," Sam screamed as he dove into the hollow. One after another, each Traveler jumped into the hollow entrance and tumbled down into its mouth. First Sam, then two of the other Travelers who were yet unknown to Judah. Pierce, Miriam, and one more of the yet unnamed Travelers jumped inside. Next, Bella and Kaija Mae were swallowed up and finally, Aviel stepped inside.

Matt carefully took all the weight of Jennifer, while Aviel put one foot inside the hollow. He took Jennifer from Matt and handed her limp body to Pierce. Judah noticed that Miriam was there as well, and he tucked himself right up beside Aviel, wedging in between his sister and Miriam.

As Jennifer was passed along to Pierce, Judah also moved, staying close to his sister. The others piled in quickly. Now, with all the Travelers, both old and new, safely inside Asphelia's Hollow, the only thing to do was wait … wait and hope they were not too late.

The cloaks were hung up on the hooks, and it was then—when they were all out in the open—that anyone got a good look at anyone else.

Pierce gently laid Jennifer down on a bench in the Eating Chamber, and Bella removed her bloodied cloak. As she did, Jennifer stirred but only slightly. Some groans slipped from the corners of her mouth and without opening her eyes, Jennifer's hand reached back behind her right ear where her wound still gaped wide.

"What should we do?" Sam asked. He knelt down beside the bloody mess of a girl and started talking so gently to her that it was honestly a little amusing. Some of the Travelers may have chuckled if the sight of the small girl laying on the bench was not so tragic.

Her lips were burned and horribly blistered. The two puncture wounds on her cheek were swollen and covered with dried blood. Her hair was full of blood from the gash behind her ear and her hands were smeared with blood from wiping her face.

Yes, this innocent little one was quite a horrendous sight to any of their eyes so indeed, no one dared to chuckle or make a peep at Sam's reaction to her. Kaija Mae stepped forward and gently pulled Jennifer's hair away from her face. Some of the long brown strands stuck to her cheek, but Kaija Mae was so gentle that it was barely noticeable.

She began rubbing her unwounded cheek and singing tenderly. It sounded like a peaceful tune, although nobody could tell for certain because the words came out in a language no one had heard before.

After a few seconds, Bella wiped the tears that were quietly spilling from her eyes. She cleared her throat and spoke softly.

"I'm going to the Cooking Chamber to get a warm cloth. Maybe if we can wipe off some of the blood, she won't be as horrified when she wakes up."

Kaija Mae stopped singing for a moment and added her own thoughts. "Yes, and perhaps the warm cloth will stir her as well." Bella stopped and turned back.

"I sure hope you are right, Kaija Mae," and with that, she disappeared into the passageway.

It Happened Like This

"Jennifer," Kaija Mae called gently. Her voice was one of the most peaceful sounds any of the Travelers had heard for quite some time —maybe ever. It had a hypnotizing effect to it. While she continued to sing quietly at first, and then louder and louder, each Traveler felt a deep comfort warm their bellies. They forgot they were hungry … or exhausted … or angry … or anxious.

"Do you know what she's singing?" Sam asked whoever's ears would hear him. A few Travelers shook their heads; some answered with a "no" and some shrugged, but it didn't matter. The effect of the song, or the voice singing it perhaps, was like a lullaby sung to a tired infant. Their eyes began to get heavy and sleep did not seem far off. It was as though the song itself had a presence that wrapped them up—swaddled them in its cadence, and begged their eyes to rest.

"Judah … Judah." The boy stirred and stretched and rubbed his eyes. Somebody was calling his name, but his eyes were so heavy—far too heavy for him to open. He didn't even try.

"Judah." The one calling to him was now shaking him slightly. "Judah, wake up," the familiar voice whispered. He began to stir more and felt something covering him. He forced his eyes open just a slit, enough to see that what was covering his warm body was a blanket; big and thick and blue. Suddenly, his mind woke enough to realize exactly where he was and why he was sleeping so soundly.

He'd been returned home and was safely in his own bed, under his own covers. Judah looked at the hand of the one who had been trying to wake him and instantly recognized the red, tattered blanket.

"Jelly Bean," he shouted and sprang out of bed. "You're OK!" Judah hugged his sister so hard she nearly lost her breath. He lifted her right off of the floor and swung her around and around.

"Judah, you're squishing me," she choked out, giggling.

"Oh, I'm sorry." He began laughing as well and gently set her back down. The excited Judah jumped up onto his bed and then back down to the floor. He could not control his laughter. His excitement was over the moon.

Judah, I have such a horrible headache … and my face hurts." Jennifer winced. "I don't remember what happened here," and as the words tumbled from her burned lips, she pulled back the hair behind her ear to reveal the deep wound. "It hurts so much Judah, what happened? I can't see it."

He laughed. "Oh Jelly Bean, I have so much to tell you," he said. "You will not believe it, but I will tell you anyway because it happened—IT ALL HAPPENED!"

His sister ran her tongue along her swollen lips and suddenly remembered how they became that way. Her fingers rubbed over the puncture wounds on her cheek.

"Oh Judah, I am such a mess," she whimpered. Her laughing stopped, and her smile faded. "I have much to tell you also, Judah, and I am sad to say that it too—though hard to believe —is all true."

At the exact moment that the twins were anticipating sharing their unbelievable-but-quite-true-indeed-stories from

Trilleah, they were interrupted by Bella's voice wafting down the hallway.

"Judah," she hollered. "Jennifer," she yelled louder. "Come to the kitchen. You've both been sleeping for nearly the entire day and you must be starving."

Jennifer looked at Judah. Judah looked at Jennifer. One stomach rumbled and then the other.

"Breakfast does sound good, don't you think, Judah?" Jennifer said. The smile did not return to her face, but she took her brother by the hand, and together they entered the hallway.

"Oh there you are, J, I've been checking on you every half hour all night and this morning. I wondered where you had gotten off to without my noticing." Bella hugged the frail girl very gently and ruffled Judah's hair. "You are quite the pair; I must say," Bella teased. "Quite the pair, indeed."

The three of them wandered hand-in-hand down the hallway and into the kitchen, Judah making very sure to keep his sister's hand wrapped tightly in his own.

"You tell your story, and then I'll tell mine," he said.

They all sat at the table—in the same places they always sat —but it seemed a bit more wonderful on this particular day.

Jennifer took a long breath in, letting the smell of whatever this was that Bella had made, linger in her nostrils. She exhaled slowly, being thankful to be sitting here, at her parents' table, smelling such wonderful smells and being with her favorite people.

"Well you see," she began, "it happened like this."

And while the young girl sat telling bits and pieces of what she had seen—and what had seen her—there was no way she could know that the moon in Trilleah was weeping … the sun was hiding itself away. Neither the sun nor the moon wanted to be witnesses to what tragedies would undoubtedly unfold if ever the Travelers were to slip back through the Gates of Solstice.

It was to be hoped, that day would never come.

… UNTIL THE NEXT JOURNEY …

The Beyond Solstice Gates Series:

1. <u>Casting Shadows</u>

   Where truth exists ... even if no one believes it.

2. <u>The Fowler's Snare</u>

   Strength is found when the eye sees
   what the heart already knows.

3. <u>Perfidy of Labyrinth</u>

   Where the only way forward is all the way back.

4. <u>Veiled Sun ✧ Blood Moon</u>

   Where the sun gives no light and the moon throws great
   drops of blood ... singing of both a great and terrible day.

5. <u>Mist Over Leviathan</u>

6. <u>War of the Firmament</u>

7. <u>Chasm of Acheron</u>